For Love of Medusa

by

Lianne Kelly

The Five Mortal Realms

For Love of Medusa

Cover Art by *Debbie Taylor*

The Wild Rose Press, Inc.
PO Box 708
Adams Basin, NY 14410-0708
Visit us at www.thewildrosepress.com

Publishing History
First Edition, 2023
Trade Paperback ISBN 978-1-5092-4790-5
Digital ISBN 978-1-5092-4791-2

The Five Mortal Realms
Published in the United States of America

"Halt, trespasser. To enter this temple means to face your doom." So melodramatic but true. She'd laugh if it wasn't so tragic.

"I've come to vanquish you, Gorgon!"

His deep voice rolled through the temple. The only thing that made his dramatic statement less cliché was his accent. From the great island of Britannia, if she had to guess.

"Vanquish? Seriously?" she teased, bored and ready to poke at the next in line for her temple decorations. "Can't you at least come up with something more original? Everyone says that."

A few steps behind a Roman centurion frozen for eternity in a most undignified pinched death face, she glimpsed movement. He was tall, in a long swishy coat with a black bag slung over his broad shoulders. Nicely proportioned. Too bad he'd be dead soon.

"Sorry my witty monster-killing repertoire is disappointing you. You speak English?"

At least this one had a sense of humor. And a nice voice, slight rough tone in contrast to a polished accent that she hadn't heard in, she guessed, a century.

"Part of my curse is knowing the language of those who enter my temple. I suppose it makes things easier for you, for them. Boring for me since all of you tend to stick to the same speech. Accusation, threat, and ignore the warning." She didn't know why she was talking to him.

"Nothing wrong with the classics." His voice had a low defensive tone with a slight edge to it.

Ah yes, the ego. Always an easy target.

Dedication

For Mom and our shared love of all things bookish

Chapter One

Medusa's curse always ended with screaming. Along with that one last gasp of breath heralding a life ended. The echoes stretched on for an eternity in the columned temple.

Every limb on fire, she stumbled back until collapsing onto the blessedly cool marble bench. Godly vengeance seared into her brain in the never-ending reminder of her curse.

Why did these trespassers keep coming? Not like they weren't warned.

She pressed fingers into her temples, easing the pounding headache of facing yet another hero or whatever they called themselves nowadays.

Formerly neat ebony braids twisted and squirmed with the evidence of her burden. The slithering mass of gold-and-green mottled snakes on her head hissed their sympathy. They were always sorry. Not as sorry as she. Or the now dead hero.

One calming breath and she opened her eyes. Yellow sunlight bounced off motes of dust hanging in the air. Her nose tickled until she released a sneeze. Hero dust. Lovely. And now she'd added another.

Waving a hand in front of her face, she stood, stretching muscles aching from another tense standoff. She'd dealt with so many intruders over the past few centuries. So many deaths and years she'd lost count.

Maybe a millennium now given the changes in style of her would-be vanquishers.

Medusa arched her back and then rolled her shoulders, almost like a cat. Even cats didn't last long around her.

Being cursed really did suck the fun out of living a long life.

As her nose itched, threatening another sneeze, she shuffled through the dimly lit temple, weaving around the cluster of statues. Well, more like former enemies who'd come to murder her. Not that any of them got very close. Idiots. Fools. All of them.

A puff of dust from one rather buff stone adversary caused another rash of sneezes. She used a fold in her chiton to wipe at her nose. Hero dust got everywhere. Keeping the place clean was impossible. They kept deteriorating all over her mosaic floors.

She bumped a stone arm, which promptly fell to the ground and shattered into rubble.

"Oh, Brutus, or was it Titus? Either way, you were a deluded hotheaded warrior. You really should have listened."

She nudged the crumbled arm aside with a gold-sandaled foot. Gods, but she needed a pedicure. Hermes was late with the latest supply delivery. And after she'd done away with that warrior competing for whatever her name was… Helen? No that was an entirely different tragedy. Maybe it was Dryope?

Medusa shrugged and continued her journey through the forest of statues, all of whom had threatened to destroy her. Like Perseus. She'd cut a deal with him that was supposed to end the nonstop carnage in her temple. It'd worked for a while.

"There you are," she murmured at her latest. "Drake of TikTok." She poked at the black rectangular device he held in his hand. "Such an odd weapon." She traced a finger down his torso, stone shirt tight against a lean frame and then trousers that stopped above his knee. "Strange fashion too."

At least sandals were back in from the look of his feet. And long hair. She did enjoy a man with flowing hair. One finger caressed the intricate sculpted waves of now stone tresses any sculptor would yearn to take credit for. Her imagination ran toward lusty memories of riding such a muscled warrior with long hair a girl could grip.

Of course, such lustful urges were behind what cursed her.

Best to avoid the heat building between her thighs. She'd spent too many nights writhing with unrelenting desire. Yearning for what she could never have—satisfaction from a partner to merge her body with until she shook from pleasure—nearly drove her mad.

She'd never fulfill such desires when everyone who even glanced at her turned to stone.

Regret and sorrow carved a hole in her chest until she craved air free of the misery so thick she could barely breathe.

The dust and cloying dank air spurred her to flee long-dead visitors. She emerged on a balcony under a sky heavy with gray clouds. A salty fresh breeze lifted her white skirts, and for a moment she basked, free from obligation and retribution. Waves crashed against the rocks beneath her, so tempting with their destructive freedom.

What she wouldn't give to swim away from this prison. Except there was no escape. Seagulls swooped and dived into the tumultuous waves. A few who dared venture too close turned to stone, plunging into the depths of Poseidon's domain. Part of her wondered if Poseidon still thought of her.

Bird droppings splatted on the stone next to her, decorating her skirts with a reminder that a goddess' wrath was eternal.

"Can you not? Isn't it enough I'm stuck on this island temple never to know the touch of another?" Probably not her best move to test Athena's temper. Last time she'd ended up with a snake-laden hairdo and cursed for all eternity.

Dainty bells chimed in the temple.

She groaned and contemplated hurling herself down onto the razor-sharp rocks. Except she doubted Athena would allow her such an easy out. No, she had to go face another alleged hero.

"Fine. You want me to destroy another life." She stomped back into the temple and fell into the routine. "Halt, trespasser. To enter this temple means to face your doom." So melodramatic but true. She'd laugh if it wasn't so tragic.

"I've come to vanquish you, Gorgon!"

His deep voice rolled through the temple. The only thing that made his dramatic statement less cliché was his accent. From the great island of Britannia, if she had to guess.

"Vanquish? Seriously?" she teased, bored and ready to poke at the next in line for her temple decorations. "Can't you at least come up with something more original? Everyone says that."

A few steps behind a Roman centurion frozen for eternity in a most undignified pinched death face, she glimpsed movement. He was tall, in a long swishy coat with a black bag slung over his broad shoulders. Nicely proportioned. Too bad he'd be dead soon.

"Sorry my witty monster-killing repertoire is disappointing you. You speak English?"

At least this one had a sense of humor. And a nice voice, slight rough tone in contrast to a polished accent that she hadn't heard in, she guessed, a century.

"Part of my curse is knowing the language of those who enter my temple. I suppose it makes things easier for you, for them. Boring for me since all of you tend to stick to the same speech. Accusation, threat, and ignore the warning." She didn't know why she was talking to him.

"Nothing wrong with the classics." His voice had a low defensive tone with a slight edge to it.

Ah yes, the ego. Always an easy target.

"Clearly, those threats didn't work for your predecessors." She prowled closer and stopped just out of his sight, her snakes softly whispering against her temples.

Her newest foe leaned in and rapped his knuckles against another poor dead warrior's shoulder.

How very out of the ordinary. And perplexing, almost to the point of intriguing her. Perhaps he wasn't cut from the same cloth as the others.

"You know, for a monster who has a reputation for terrorizing and murdering, you certainly have opinions about those sent to defeat you. Shouldn't you be attacking by now?"

"For someone eager to die, you seem to be taking your time looking around," she tartly noted, even though she quite enjoyed a verbal assault over the normal swords, spears, and various other weapons.

Even in the dim light, she caught him smile until his cheek dimpled.

"Can't argue with such sound logic."

His voice, the low tone and how he drew out his words, resonated and hit a soft spot. She shouldn't allow herself to cuddle up to the column, flushing with feelings she'd banished so long ago. Although nothing wrong with a pre-death conversation to lull him to his end. It was so much better than screaming horror.

"Maybe if you followed logic, you wouldn't be here. This is my home. You do realize you're the trespasser."

She kept to the shadows, watching him trace his fingers along the screaming stone face of another dead warrior. Curiosity and compassion oozed from this one.

"Fair point." He inclined his head and slid back a step. "This isn't exactly going like I thought. So do you study us before the whole cursing?"

"Not really. But I think we've established you're not like the others. Would it disappoint you to learn I didn't ask for this job and the never-ending confrontation? I was just having some fun when things got out of hand."

"Out of hand," he muttered, and then silence stretched until he dropped the black bag.

The soft thud didn't have the clank of a shield or sword. But weapons had changed over the centuries. Rolling her bottom lip with a perplexed confusion, she moved silently, like her often-written-about serpentine hair, until she hovered behind a trio of toga-wearing warriors forever screaming in death.

They were so different from her current intruder. He raked a hand through shoulder-length steel-gray hair. He didn't turn toward her, much to his good fortune.

"It's punishment for me as well as you." She didn't say it with as much anger as usual, but then this was an odd day for her.

"I'm sorry. I didn't think—"

"Well, that's clear. You didn't heed the warnings. And you're not much of a warrior if you don't mind me saying."

"No," he drew out and again fidgeted and frowned, grabbing her broom, which she had left lying about. She didn't exactly have people over for tea, but tidying the temple relieved boredom. Every muscle locked, and even her snakes seemed to gape as he swept the floor and smiled.

"You're cleaning me to death?"

"Sorry, it's just all of this..." He swept an arm before him. "It's my life's work, studying the mythology and cultural impact of the Olympian pantheon on society. Your existence on this island proves we got it wrong. Turns the whole Perseus story on its ear."

"Perseus had one job. Parade around and brag to give me some peace, and he couldn't even do that!"

"The old stories never mentioned this pre-death chat either," he confided. "Annoying when the sources turn out unreliable." He laid the broom against a statue and wandered through the temple, gazing up at the ceiling as much as he paid homage to her victims. She caught one murmured *bloody brilliant*.

Reality again hit her that she was conversing with a soon-to-be victim. Only, maybe she didn't want to end this one.

He reached the perimeter where sunlight dappled, highlighting crumbling statues and a few smashed amphora, wine long since dried up.

7

"You know, on a scale of screaming and storming my temple to giving me the not-so-clever quips about how monstrous I am, this rates a solid ten for you lasting as long as you have. Well done, you." Humor wasn't her normal, but neither was he.

"Thanks. Wait, you rate us?" He shrugged his coat off, then slung it over a half-destroyed statue. He paused, gaze focused on the floor. Pulling out black-rimmed glasses, he then knelt to examine the mosaic tiles.

A wave of amusement flushed through her, and she crept closer.

Sunlight cast its golden glow against his face, revealing ocean-blue eyes. A smooth jaw and he had an aquiline nose resembling one of the noble Olympians. Not as young as most who came for her, but he had a strength and energy in how he moved.

He had an Olympian esthetic for sure. All he needed was a tunic and golden laurel crown. Heat flushed down to her thighs. Just her type. The impossible temptation.

"Your temple is gorgeous. It's a perfect example of high classical Ionic design. Pentelic marble. Magnificent sculptures. The ones carved, not cursed. I could spend months sketching and never capture the artistry."

He wouldn't last months. The fantasy of having this gorgeous mortal in her temple, talking with her, made her heart beat a little faster and heat flush her neck. Even her snakes hissed quietly and didn't do their typical curse thrashing.

"No one comes here to admire a falling-apart temple. Shouldn't you be hunting me by now?"

He paused and rubbed a finger in the corner of his right eye. "About that…I might have exaggerated a bit."

"Well, that's a new one," she admitted and moved

deeper into the shadows, then settled on a bench to enjoy the adorable way he pulled off his glasses and shoved them into his shirt pocket. A button-up shirt, she noted, untucked and hanging over jeans, which gave her pause.

Hermes provided her with enough reading material from this mortal realm to give her an inkling about modern attire, and she did enjoy how his jeans fit, giving her a nice view of his manly features.

"I'm a professor," he announced after standing and wiping his hands on his jeans. "I've studied ancient Greek culture for so long, and to see it…to meet you is just everything. Blimey, I'm mucking this up." He tipped his head back, giving her a nice glimpse of a muscular neck.

"What I mean is in the modern world it's all social media and disrespect of just about everything. We lack the nobility of exploration, quests, and great thinkers of the ancient world. And now I've found you, one of the best of the old stories. It's an honor to face you, even if it's not exactly a battle. Not that I want to fight you. Although I've been told I talk enough to suck the life out of my students."

He complimented her. And she enjoyed the charming babble. Especially when delivered by a gorgeous male specimen. A mortal one, but no one was perfect.

Her stomach twisted into a knot at this complication. What did she do with this? She didn't converse with mortals. Ever. Yet there she was and starting to have a few fantasies on top of it all.

She eyed the enormous statue of Athena, dominating this end of the temple. This had to be a test. Or torture.

Chapter Two

"Uh, Miss Medusa?"

Stunned and amused appeared to be the theme of her morning. Also charmed by her odd intruder who squeezed his eyes shut and muttered, "Disrespectful," before continuing. "Noble Gorgon?" A tentative inquiry echoed in a way no other had before.

"Maybe you should stick with Medusa." Now she was on familiar terms with him, and didn't that fluster her snakes? This talking with him also fluttered in her chest. Except this would end in his death no matter how beguiling he was. And yet part of her yearned to prolong their conversation. "If you don't mind me asking, what's your name? I like to know what to call you when you've turned into one of my stone decorations."

Her snakes hissed, "Liiiaarrr." She shushed them and their honesty.

"Jason Walker. And it's an honor to meet you." He bowed and swept his arm out in a courtly gesture.

"It's been lovely meeting you, Jason Walker. You're the nicest intruder to enter my temple in a long while. I'm sorry I have to end you. Try not to scowl while you die. You have such a lovely face, and it would be a shame to ruin it for eternity."

She flinched and bent forward, pressing her hands to her face to stifle a groan. *Yes, badly flirt him to death. That's the way to do it.* Even the hissing mass of her curse flopped down on her shoulders in disappointment.

"You've got a point. Terrible way to end. Mind if I look around first?" An amused lilt in his voice lifted the normally murky atmosphere. He nonchalantly strolled toward the very balcony she'd stood on earlier. Bathed in the light, he swept his gaze across the ocean horizon. "Not a bad view," he called over his shoulder before withdrawing back into the shadowed interior, again pausing to squint at the stone warriors.

"You know, the ferryman'll be pleased not to see me again. He's got a bit of an attitude. Could use a shot of something to lighten up. He wasn't in any of the written accounts either. And I've read all of them. Even Ovid's. He was sympathetic to you. Did you know him?" He continued his amble around, poking at petrified heroes until one lost a nose, which at least made him pause.

She stifled a giggle as he picked it up and tried to stick it back on before shoving it in his pocket.

"I suppose we should get on with the cursing. I've left instructions with the innkeeper on the main island, and blimey, this is awkward. Anyway—" He cleared his throat and peered into the shadows.

The first thought pounding in her veins was *no, not yet*.

"Jason Walker, why did you come here to die?" In all her cursed centuries, she'd never thought to ask.

He blinked, and his brow pinched in an adorable confusion. "I didn't just come here to die," he said slowly, heaving a sigh before he walked to his black bag and knelt beside it. "I've mucked this up royally. I mean, sure, dying was part of being here, but it was more about the discovery and proving everyone else wrong." His voice turned bitter, and a scowl marred his features before he tugged a piece of metal until the bag opened.

A burning nausea sat in the pit of her stomach. Despite what he said, dread chilled her spine. Was he reaching for a weapon? He seemed so nice, and…there it was. She liked this mortal. More than liked him.

He pulled out a book.

Her blood sang, and the temple practically spun around her as she was thrust into a state of chaotic disbelief. Not a weapon, but literature. She wanted to laugh. Maybe she'd finally gone mad.

"It's not exactly a best seller. Even my university wouldn't let me put it on the curriculum, but it might give you a laugh in how wrong the modern world sees your world."

If this was madness, she was all for it. Girlish excitement fluttered at not a weapon, but a gift. Drawn to him and wary of her curse, she slid off her bench and ducked around Athena's statue for a closer look. The hard-covered book he held was nice, but the real treat was how his light-blue shirt unbuttoned enough to reveal an expanse of neck and muscled chest. Gods, what she wouldn't give to— She never finished that thought as he rambled on.

"You don't have to read it. I mean, it's nothing compared to where you're from. Maybe we should get to the cursing part. Like I said, I've made arrangements and don't have anything to get back to. My work will be published, and that's that."

"I don't want to end you." She'd never spoken truer words. "You've shown kindness and intelligence I've not known in all my years in this temple. In return for your courtesy, I can give you the one thing I can't have. A life outside this temple."

"Life out there isn't all that. It's hard and judgmental."

He turned abruptly, and Medusa only barely dove out of his line of sight, bumping into one of her more annoying would-be vanquishers. Sir Harold of Wales, she thought he was. Dressed in strange metal plates, he'd been noisy and not at all courteous like Jason.

"You're a scholar, one who learns and passes on knowledge. Sounds like something your world needs."

"No one back home will miss me. After I lost my parents, my brother and I couldn't get along, and I didn't seem to fit in anywhere, not even at uni. Finding you, ending in this place until I become just so much dust, fits." His voice had lowered, still deep but resonating with a flat sadness. Until a gentle breeze swirled dust in the air around him, and he sneezed.

"Hero dust. It's not good for the complexion or your nose." She tried teasing him.

"I never thought of that." He frowned and rubbed at his nose, the shirt pulling tight against shoulders.

Medusa stood in the shadow of the grand statue of Athena who had made her the monster she was, and her thoughts turned toward how Athena represented wisdom, courage, and justice. Unleashing her curse on Jason didn't seem just. Despite his declarations of having nothing in his world, he had so much to offer. She could tell that after the short time she'd known him.

"Jason, I don't have many friends. You feel like one. Please don't make me kill a friend." Her voice lowered to a soft lyrical cadence with her very real need to save him. "You could go home and write a new story, an epic tale of how you won over this gorgon with kind words. How you learned that even a monster has feelings and suffers loneliness and regrets. Wouldn't it make a better story if someone lived?"

"I'm so sorry."

Three words she hadn't heard from anyone in centuries, if ever. Her throat thickened with a strange emotion welling through her in hot waves.

So much for the fierce angry gorgon meting out retribution for her unfair curse.

"The world's not fair to any of us." His words hung in the air with wisdom. "I'm no better than any of these coming here, making demands on you. I should know better. I bloody read all the great thinkers in the ancient text." He waved his arms around and tilted his head back, barking out a hard laugh. "I'm so thick! It's as clear as day. You were a victim lashing out. You are, aren't you?" He stepped forward, peering into the darkness cloaking her.

She withdrew as far as she could, unwilling to end him. Or ruin how much they connected just talking.

"No mortal could understand me or my pain. Your life is as brief as a sunset, barely grasping your own existence until it's over." She slumped down into a corner, in subservience at Athena's statue. A place she knew too well after years of begging for forgiveness. She flicked crumbled marble and drew symbols in the dirt, ancient runes from her childhood while he continued their conversation.

"Trust me, doesn't feel like a blink of an eye. I wouldn't be here if it did. But I understand loneliness and pain. But I don't mean to add to yours."

"I told you, you can go home. Go back to the world, your family, and life, boasting how you survived. Get your reward and acclaim. Do it before I change my mind."

"But that's the thing. I don't have anything to go home to. Don't have a home anymore. Like I said, my parents are gone. Don't have any kids. And never married. My arsehole department head ended my tenure on some ethics rule, citing my radical theories. And that one time I protested the uni admissions policy. He might have been right. No place for me there, and nothing much left to do with my life other than this."

Although she didn't understand everything he said, the bitterness, being treated unfairly and a world turned against him, sank into the pit of burning resentment she'd thought would never die. Empathy swelled in her chest until for one moment her regrets lay in how she couldn't offer him comfort. A hug would only kill him, and that she would not have. She stood and rubbed the dirt off her hands on her gown.

"Jason, I need you to do something for me." Her palms grew damp with nerves. Her snakes itched at her scalp, unaccustomed to being denied. They'd already had their due earlier. Or maybe they reminded her she needed to be more than a victim of her curse.

"I don't know what I could do for you." He sounded baffled.

"Live." She reached down into a basket, one of the tributes to Athena, and pulled out a coin that she tossed in the air, arcing to land at his feet. "Take it and give it to Charon for passage home. Tell my story to those who'll listen. Maybe they'll stop coming. If you're my friend, you'll do this for me. Help me, Jason. Be my hero."

She swore the ground shook at her uttering. Probably blasphemous. Especially in her family.

"I'm not the hero type. I mean look at me here." He spread his arms wide. "Not quite battle ready. Not that I can't hold my own on the street or a pub brawl, but I'm no Achilles."

"Achilles was overrated and had divine help thanks to his mother. A true hero seeks out destiny, risking his mortal life." She might have romanticized that last part just a touch.

"A true hero doesn't do things for his own benefit. Part of me being here is a bit of an ego thing, to be published and recognized. To be honest, I'm sort of an egotistical wanker at work and socially. Even my students gave me rubbish reviews, complaining I get off topic and my exams are too vague. I even checked out too many library books and kept forgetting to pay the fines until they banned me."

"I have no idea what all that is, but it's better than here. Now, please do this for me. As a favor."

Favors had consequences. She felt it at the hissing cackle of her snakes. Never good.

"What if I spend that life here? I could be your advocate, chasing intruders away from you. Like a knight. You know what those are, right?"

"Such a hero already." She sighed, not entirely understanding but her heart growing soft and gooey over a man with such a lovely voice and noble intent. "The world deserves a man like you to be out there living. Not here among the dead. Oh, Jason, you gave me the best day, and I'll think of you often, your true heart and how you chose to listen. Remember that. Nothing is as attractive as a man who listens. Goodbye, Jason."

Medusa channeled her anger and annoyance, the curse of her retribution, into the elements in the temple.

Her body itched, and her skin grew tight and hot, unleashing herself in a burst of power as if Athena herself raged. The temple shook before wind gusted and tossed Jason out, rolling him down the hill toward the cranky ferryman who would not be happy to have his nap interrupted.

Exhausted and emotionally drained, she collapsed onto the dusty floor. One good deed hardly made up for all the lives she'd taken. She looked over to find his bag. Mementos of one good man who didn't meet a tragic end.

Chapter Three

Jason tumbled arse over kettle until he landed in a heap at the end of the dirt path that led to Medusa's home. Like a phantom taunting him on his failure, his long coat whipped in the wind, chasing him, until it slammed into his face.

"Bloody hell." He tugged it off and winced at whatever he'd landed on. Coat thrown aside, he pulled a jagged shard of marble from under his arse, then tossed it into the tall weeds and scraggly brush.

"Can't even die properly." He dug his hiking boots into the ground and kicked out at rocks and sand before rubbing at torn denim over his knee. "Offering her my book like she'd want to read it. Daft pillock." The whole thing had been a romantic concept. A quest for truth. Die in the throes of proving his theories.

A tarnished gold coin glinted in gravel and dirt next to him. Medusa had sent him on his way without a glimpse of the gorgon he'd read so much about. And with a lesson on how the legends barely scraped the surface of who she really was. He didn't deserve her kindness.

He scooped up the coin and held it up to the light. Grit covered the surface. He swiped his thumb over the raised face of Apollo. Tangible evidence he'd spent more than a decade of his life looking for. Yet all he could think about was the tragedy of Medusa.

A gust of wind whistled through barren trees, taunting him with his former heroic ideals. How the mighty professor and his old-world ideals of heroes had fallen. Pride firmly battered and bruised, he clambered up, yanking his coat with him. The only positive of this day lay in the fact Medusa's existence proved his theory about the Olympian gods. And that the mad ramblings he'd been accused of by his brother, his department head, and anyone else who deemed themselves an intellect were proven true.

A cold raindrop splashed on his forehead. He squinted against the very real and not mythological potential downpour threatening from the dark-gray clouds. Years of frustration erupted at what he perceived as another godly roadblock. He jammed his arm into his coat.

"I know you're out there, all of you that toy with us mortals. I haven't forgotten what you did to my parents."

A gust of rain stung his face, the water sliding down his neck in a mocking chill until he lifted an arm to shield his face. Maybe it was the gods trying to chase him away from the gorgon who spared his life. Or his accusation hit a little too close to home. Peering into the swirling dark-gray clouds, he took satisfaction at that. Until the enormity of his presence and what he'd done that day stole some of his proverbial thunder.

"She deserves better." An obvious statement. He snorted at himself. Doing a lot of that lately. Time to tell destiny to piss off. He could almost hear the swell of a heroic score of music when the hero made his story-altering choice. He rather liked that analogy. Even if he had initially failed the hero part.

"Medusa." Her name no longer meant death. She

had an enchanting voice, deep and velvety like a caress. Even now, he felt warmth slide through him at how she teased and confronted him. Nothing like the string of exes whose lives he never quite fit. Which had been fine by him.

Apparently, he preferred older women of the mythological sort. Which all but settled what he'd do next. He'd give Medusa her proper due, more than idiots attacking or looking for fame and fortune.

Thunder rumbled, and the rain fell with a force that left him shivering. No doubt the gods tested him. Fine by him.

Scowling, he grabbed his coat and quickly shrugged into it. As the sky rumbled, he glanced back at the tall, crumbling edifice of the temple, mist rising up from the sea to once again cloak its existence. Pounding drops soaked through his coat until his muscles ached from shaking. It didn't matter. He had a new quest, one that invigorated him with confidence.

Clambering and skidding down the steep path to the dock, he found his ride leaning heavily on a staff, the wind whipping at his long black cloak.

"Oi, what are you doing alive?" The ferryman's voice was raspy and accusatory as he wrapped one gray-and-white boney hand around his staff. "This is against the rules. You visit, die, and I ferry your soul to the Underworld."

"Not today, mate. I need a lift back to the beach." Pumped with adrenaline at his discovery, he almost laughed at the madness of chatting with a ferryman of the Underworld.

"Well, that's gonna cost you for mucking about with my quota and reputation. What'll the boys on the Styx say when I come back empty-handed?"

Jason held up the coin.

"Is that stolen?" A bony pointed chin protruded from the heavy black hood.

"It's compensation. Now let's shift." He tossed the coin at the ferryman who caught it midair.

"Highly irregular. I'll be filing a complaint."

"You do that." Jason climbed onto the rickety wooden skiff while the grumbling ferryman pushed them into the angry sea.

Medusa had called him Charon, and Jason would have been keen to push the subject with him if not for the weather. Waves churned and tossed them around until Jason's stomach rolled. He was a tough bastard in most environments, but not the ocean.

Further evidence the whole hero thing seemed doubtful. He clamped a white-knuckled grip on the wooden edge of the skiff until, mercifully, they crashed into the dock.

"Go on, back to the living." The ferryman's rough voice carried on the gusting wind, sea spray whipping at his black robes.

"Thanks for the ride." Jason swung himself out onto the creaking wooden dock. His muscles ached with each drenched step. No one said a quest was easy, but blimey, he could do with a little less misery. He swept his drenched hair away from his face and swiped rain from his eyes before glancing over his shoulder at the ferryman. "I'll be back tomorrow."

"Course you will. All you mortals need my services eventually."

The wind howled along the shoreline, forcing Jason to stumble back a step, one arm covering his face until he hit solid land. Gritting his teeth against the downpour, he made for the only way off the beach, a steep path leading to the top of the hill.

Cold sliced through him until his teeth chattered at each step up slippery rocks and earth. Thunder rumbled so loud it seemed to vibrate through his bones. No doubt, the pantheon of gods were having at him. He gripped the branch of a barren tree and hauled himself up the last few feet to his parked moped.

He breathed hard as rain continued to sting at his face even as excitement pounded in his veins with the realization of what he'd accomplished.

"I lived!" he shouted and leapt up, pumping his fist. "You hear that, world! I was ready to pop off in the name of research. But I was right, they exist, all of them, and one thinks I'm worth saving!" Lightning carved through sky. He had enough self-preservation to duck down next to his moped.

No sense tempting fate. He had work ahead of him before he returned to Medusa. He spared one final glance at the Aegean, once again shrouding Medusa's Island in mist, hiding it from the world.

But not from him. He'd gained more than proof that day. Funny thing, life, giving him answers but also leaving him wanting more. Not to die, but to spend more time with the most intriguing woman he'd ever met.

If…he didn't die on the trip back to the village. With his luck on the dodgy moped, that was entirely possible.

The storm followed him as he made the journey down treacherous, winding roads to the tiny village of Pacheia. Despite buffeting winds, he didn't crash until he arrived in town. The bumpy pebble-strewn road combined with puddles made for a messy skid and semi-crash to a parking space. Against sluicing rain, he trudged into the hole-in-the-wall bar and inn, the Golden Bow.

"Jason lives! We were making wagers on whether you'd make it back alive. I guess the gods must be favoring you." The innkeeper let loose a growling laugh from behind the wooden bar that lined the dimly lit room.

"Something like that." Jason ignored him and peeled off his coat. He dropped it on a chair before warming his hands near the meager fireplace surrounded by cracked plaster walls.

Only a couple of local fishermen, drowning their sorrows, sat at one of the rickety wooden tables in the cramped, low-ceilinged room.

"Come on, lad, let's make a toast." The innkeeper and sometimes bartender, Erik, rounded the bar and clamped a hand on his shoulder. Cold, exhausted, and coming off an adrenaline high, Jason collapsed into a chair at the table closest to the fire next to the innkeeper who he'd learned was an expat from Croydon.

A steaming mug that had a hint of something other than tea was shoved at him by a dark-haired woman with a permanent glare fixed on her face. A bowl of lamb stew and bottle of the local spirits followed.

"Go on, eat. Then give me a good story. You were gone all day." Erik leaned back, swallowing a shot of the inn's home brew.

"Not much to tell." Jason evaded giving too many details. "Spent some time studying the ruins in the south and then followed a trail down to the shore. Got a lift to one of the volcanic islands and nearly drowned when the storm blew in." The tea scorched a trail into his belly. He managed not to cough and tore into the stew.

Would Medusa like stew? He should bring her a picnic, maybe some chocolate to make up for bumbling into her home and being a pompous arse.

Erik leaned in close and pushed the empty shot glass with one blunt-tipped finger. "So you went by sea, did ya? You saw the temple."

Jason nearly choked on his meal.

Wavy blond hair down to his shoulders, Erik grinned and shook his head. "You think you're the first? Come on. Like the locals don't know or haven't made a few quid off tourists bumbling around out there."

Jason shoved the bowl aside. "If you knew it was there, why'd you tell me I was better off on the tourist trail in Athens and Delphi?"

"Wanted to see how far you were willing to go." Erik poured another shot and downed it, followed by a sharp inhale. "I had to be sure. It's dangerous and not for the casual lot or glory seekers. The last thing we need is reality TV or more of the social-media types here. You do know what's in the temple." His smile slipped, and the sound of the wind battering the door eased.

"Tragedy is in that temple. And maybe a chance for the right person to do something about it." His brother always said he had a gob on him and especially after drinking. But Erik had said the villagers knew about the island.

His gaze swept the room. A few people slipped into the pub. Friendly chatter and the clink of glasses followed. They didn't look like the types to hide the biggest find in the modern world. Or the most dangerous.

Except the innkeeper. And maybe the waitress, Petra, who never once attempted to chat him up. Not that he was looking, but he'd grown accustomed to social niceties like flirting and looking to sell a few more drinks. She'd eyed him with suspicion since the day he arrived.

Unlike Erik who now winked at Petra as she passed before he leveled an assessing gaze at Jason. An odd warmth crawled up his neck at the scrutiny. Followed by a flutter in his abdomen and he began questioning what was in that drink. He caught a twitch of a smile from Erik who then rubbed a hand over his smooth tanned jaw before pouring another shot.

"There is tragedy in that temple, but you're still here. And I've got to say, of all the tourists hunting treasure and such in these waters, you never struck me as the heroic type hell-bent on running to your death."

"I'm not. I just—" Spiked tea seemed a good distraction. A swallow stole his breath. "How the hell do you drink this stuff?" he coughed out, the fire in his belly traveling to his head.

"You dropped off a mysterious package and a will, being all dramatic and enigmatic." Erik leaned closer, tapping his forefinger on the table at each point. "Left us all atwitter. Petra thought we should hand it over to the local coppers. Not that they care without a body. So tell me, mate, why are you really here? And don't give me research and a holiday." He shoved the bottle across the battered wooden table, his oxford gaping, revealing a golden bow-and-arrow amulet around his neck.

Maybe the drink skewed his perception. Or learning everything he'd studied and dreamed about was real, but Jason's tongue loosened, and his judgment disappeared in a swish of alcohol.

"I'm tired of being ridiculed, of being an outcast for dedication to my work and asking the questions those stick-up-their-arses types won't." He took another drag of the spiked tea. He sucked in air and lifted his head. The ceiling suddenly tilted, and he grabbed the edge of the table.

"So you told everyone to piss off and came here," Erik prompted.

"I don't care about them. I came here because I wanted to find proof that my theories about the immortals and their stories are real. That there are forces out there influencing our lives even if most deny it. Even if it ended me. What better way to die than a pursuit of knowledge and truth?"

"Cheers to nobility." Erik tilted his head and sipped his drink. "So clearly, you avoided the death part of this project. Did you find your passion, proof that Jason Walker isn't a complete whackadoo?"

"Maybe I did. But not like I thought. History, journals, archaeological evidence, and all that lot only tells part of the story." Half pissed, exhausted, and with his mind spinning from discovery, Jason leaned an elbow on the table. "Turns out I was wrong. Forgot to remember history is all personal accounts filled with human errors and prejudice. They called her a monster, but the truth is we're the monsters, and we need to learn to do better." More tea burned past his lips.

"You really found her." Erik's voice softened, and his chair scraped across the gritty wooden floor.

Jason smelled a sweet cologne like honeysuckle that mixed with the alcohol of the drink.

"And you lived. Now, how'd you manage that?"

"We talked. She has a nice voice, all sultry like. Maybe part siren, you know? You can hear it when she smiles or is sad." His words slurred as a heavy warmth spread to his limbs. "I've read all about her, and I think Ovid got it right. She was gorgeous and not like the other gorgons. A timeless beauty inside and out. Even with the snakes and curse. She's compassionate and lonely. It's not fair."

Erik went quiet, and Jason's eyelids grew heavy. He scrubbed at his face, stifling a yawn.

"I'm gonna go back and see her tomorrow. Just need a nap and work out a plan. And presents. Got to bring her gifts, er, tribute. Don't tell anyone. Got be shhhhh." He tried to bring his finger to his lips but kept hitting his nose.

"Are you asking for my help and blessing?"

Jason thought that an odd question but had difficulty doing more than grunting a slurred *maybe* before finding the table irresistible. Sinking toward the wooden surface, he struggled to keep his eyes open.

"You'll have it, if only for entertainment value. Also, might be a good challenge to see this through. But mainly, it's to stir up the old guard. Jason, my lad, I promise you this one is going to turn all the Olympian gossips on their ear. I might even get a lecture."

Jason opened one eye, confused by whatever the innkeeper kept blogging on about. Then Erik's face seemed to blur and shimmer. He swore he saw a laurel crown on his head right before Jason plummeted into a blissful abyss.

Darkness turned into the ocean taking his parents and an aching loss. Except somewhere in the murkiness of his dreams was a husky voice asking him to live for her. He jerked awake to cold water dripped down his neck.

"There he is. Wakey, wakey. You'll never make it

27

into the legends if you sleep one off here."

Jason pried himself off the table. "What time is it?" His throat burned, and even the dim yellow light in the bar hurt his eyes. He squinted, and his stomach rolled.

"What day is it, you mean!" Erik slapped him on the shoulder before dropping a worn leather-covered book in front of him. "It's a record of those who came before you. Read it. Maybe you'll learn something, and if she lets you live again, I'll introduce you to the local seer who I nicked it from. She's a bit of a character but makes a wicked lemon cake. Best get cleaned up. Even a gorgon has taste, and you reek."

Unable to do more than grunt, Jason grabbed what was more of a handwritten journal. He stumbled toward the stairs, wincing as Erik whistled behind the bar.

A list of Medusa's assassins didn't interest him. Her history and what made her into the gorgon that let him go did. Erik was right about one thing. She deserved better than him smelling like yesterday's rubbish.

Chapter Four

"Dates, nuts, and, oh gods, not more oranges. I'm so sick of fruit." Medusa aimed the orange abomination at the head of Don Rodrigo de Castillo. Or what was left of his formerly clanking, loud self. He crumbled slightly at the impact.

"That was as disappointing as you were." She kicked one of the baskets of tribute that Hermes hurled down before dashing off that morning. "At least there's fresh linens, modern books, and an odd-looking tablet." She held up the metallic rectangle, which chimed and glowed before she tossed it aside.

Mortals and their clever inventions often amused her. But more appealing was Jason's book and his black bag, the contents of which she'd unabashedly riffled through.

For a man about to die, his prized possessions were nothing like what she'd expect. When she knelt, peering inside, she'd found an assortment of books. She slid out one large-sized paperback and settled on the floor cross-legged. As she paged through, she found wrong assumptions about Hellenistic Greek culture amusing. But her amusement was cut short when a picture tucked in the pages fell out. It was of an older couple, a younger version of Jason, and another young man. Both with dark graying hair.

"You see, you do have a life." The image gave her

pause at digging through his personal things. The reminder of family sat like a lump in her throat. She carefully slipped it between the pages and then set the book aside.

She should stop and let him and curiosity about his life go. Except she already might be in too deep and had already begun a deep dive into his things. No sense stopping now. She dragged the bag into her lap and continued her survey of what the modern man carried on his quest. Crinkly plastic water bottles were set aside until she found a tarnished silver flask with a fiery drink she all but spit out.

The best find was the softest, thickest navy tunic with a hood. It smelled woodsy yet enticing like sunlight warming lilacs. Wrapped in the tunic was a flat metal item, similar to the one delivered by Hermes. But also, a tablet of paper with sketches of her, temples, glyphs, and creatures from the other realms she knew well.

Unable to resist, she wrapped his tunic around her shoulders and went to her alcove to enjoy his sketches. Thoughts of Jason and what he held precious had plagued her lonely night. Curled up with his tunic, she'd burned with fantasies for him. Jason, his thick, luscious hair curled around his neck and his low rough voice, had kept her writhing and burning with fantasies, imagining him beneath her. An impossible dream.

Her punishment grew worse, it seemed.

The gentle tinkling warning bells interrupted her mooning. Another day, another intruder to punish. Until she heard the voice from her fantasies.

"Hallo, it's Jason."

Well, that took the vengeance right out of her before she uttered the warning.

He'd come back. She was overcome with a compulsion to straighten her dress and threaten her snakes into submission. It was fine. No big deal. The racing of her heart was merely her reaction to the bells. Had nothing to do with the echo of his voice or that she had another chance to enjoy this mad, gorgeous mortal.

"I told you to leave and save yourself." She tried to add a sternness to her voice, but Goddess help her, she couldn't. She tossed a blanket over his tunic. "Why did you come back?"

"For you, of course. And me. Yesterday, when we talked, I started to think about what you said about living and life. Here's you, suffering, stuck in this temple. And I'm being the prat professor swanning in with no regard for you beyond what I wanted to believe."

Carrying a large basket, he wound his way around stone statues, pigeons beating their wings in the rafters at his progress. Each time he dipped and swayed around long-dead adversaries, she found her lips parting in a sigh.

She skulked among the shadows, creeping closer to enjoy the view. Today's treat was a tight midnight-blue shirt, stretched against a lightly muscled chest. And he was still talking. She should really listen instead of ogle from the darkness.

"I deserved a good cursing. Been cursed plenty by my brother and university colleagues," he said, stopping not far from Athena's statue, toeing aside crumbled marble. "Never thought I'd be as bad as them, but here we are. So this is me making amends for being an idiot. You deserve to have some of that life you wanted for me. Mates, friends, don't abandon each other to suffer. I've got lunch. Maybe we can set aside the whole vengeance

31

and turning me to stone for a while."

Gods help her. She compulsively tugged at the folds of skirts and darted looks at him. He set the basket down and opened it. He had really lovely hands. And he'd brought gifts. Her heart skipped a beat, and part of her wanted to dance. Yes, her, the gorgon who'd slayed hundreds, wanted to spin and sashay her hips. For once, a man didn't come to slay her but pay her court.

Unless she was wrong.

The heat in her cheeks ebbed as oil lanterns creaked and swung in the breeze. When she looked around, the brief elation faded. Damp, dusty stone temple in a perpetual state of decay wasn't exactly romantic.

She was surrounded by a saturation of death. Not a place where anyone came to do anything like woo. And she was the most un-wooable creature in the five mortal realms.

Well, maybe her sister Stheno, but last she heard, her sister had made a home in another of the five realms and hooked up with a dragon immune to her curse. No dragons in Earth Realm. Not that Medusa had a yearning for a scaly lover. She liked the human, tall, scruffy kind.

"You shouldn't have come back, Jason. This isn't a place for mortals."

"I think we established yesterday I haven't done well in the land of the living. Don't mind if I hang out here for a while. Besides, I'm on holiday and don't have anywhere else to be. I hope you like roast chicken. The innkeeper kitted me out with a picnic. There's bread, cheese, tomatoes, wine, and I found some biscuits and chocolate bars, although no guarantee they aren't stale."

"Did you say chocolate? The divine food of the gods?"

Medusa stood speechless. Her snakes coiled tightly in her braids, hissing in delight at an actual meal that didn't include fruit and the few fish she managed to catch that didn't turn to stone.

Jason had won over her curse with some decent protein. But even better, he'd brought her a treat she never hoped to taste again.

"Chocolate's a thing on Olympus?" He paused in shaking out a white cloth and tossing his coat over a statue.

Medusa giggled. A true girlish feminine sound that tickled her chest. Certainly not the hiss or monstrous threat she was known for. She watched him snap with great flourish what was surely a tablecloth and lay it on the ground.

"Yes, chocolate is treasured. I tasted it once when I was a girl and never thought I would again. You didn't need to do all this. And you know I can't—"

Athena's statue stood ominously over them both. A heavy reminder picnics and romance were not for her.

"Ye of little faith. I, in my astounding intellect, figured out we can eat and chat but don't have to see each other. I even picked up a little something to bribe the ferryman." He unpacked the basket, spreading out a meal that made her salivate.

Once again, this mortal had won her over with his kindness as much as his conversation.

"And what did you bribe Charon with?"

"He really is Charon?" He rolled up his sleeves and swept back his hair into a ponytail. "I thought you and the innkeeper were pulling one over on me. So how come Charon's here and not ferrying the dead?"

Warmth spread low in her abdomen. A thick manly

neck beckoned her to nibble. His rolled-up sleeves revealed strong, tanned arms, more manly than Heracles himself. At least to her. Jason might not be a young stallion, but he was better. Solid, self-assured, and noble. Better than chocolate. She squeezed her thighs together as all new fantasies emerged.

"It's an agreement with Hades. Charon works across the five mortal realms. Usually, when he brings people here, they don't survive, and he takes their souls to Hades. I'm sure he wasn't excited about a living mortal returning for a ride. You said an innkeeper knows of Charon?"

An itch of suspicion crawled up her neck as she listened.

"Erik's an expat who shipwrecked on the island ten years ago. Him and his island brew seem good at collecting secrets from thirsty travelers. Like how many visitors disappear into the ocean mist or that Charon has a taste for orange fizz."

Of course the outside world knew something of her. If it didn't, she wouldn't have so many stone reminders of her curse. However…having them know specifically of Charon or keeping records of who visited made her snakes hiss with a touch of wariness. This reeked of Olympian influence.

She clenched her jaw at the thought of who might have influenced Jason and what twisted plans might be in the works.

"Picnic done." He stood, hands on his hips, and inspected what he'd laid out. "Sorry about the plastic cups for the wine, it was best I could do. I'll just leave everything out for you. I mean, is there some ceremony when someone brings you an offering?"

Once again, his obliviousness to how much danger he was in brought her back from the edge of suspicion and retribution against interfering Olympians.

"No one offers me anything. This is the Temple of Athena. I usually make do with offerings made to her or whatever Hermes drops off." She should press him on this innkeeper but not at the chance she might cause his doom. Tucked away in the shadows, she stood rigid as anxiety squeezed at her chest.

"This isn't safe for you. None of it, you or whoever on this island is influencing you."

"Oh, I've thought of that," he drew out. "It's not like I haven't seen enough to suspect the possibility of otherworldly forces messing in my life. It's not like I don't see signs and portents in the outside world. But me being here is a dream and a choice. How about we agree I'll keep to myself over near the sunlight, and we can talk?"

"But what if you turn and I—" The thought crushed her deep in a place she'd long thought dead. In such a short time, Jason had given her hope. It compelled her to once again pray to the gods to end the curse that had taken so many lives. Even if it meant ending her life. And if they were influencing him, the thought twisted in her belly worse than fear of what she might do.

"Even if I turned to stone, I'd have no regrets. This here with you is the best time I've had in more years than I can count."

Medusa's cheeks heated, and her heart raced. So many centuries alone and bitter were erased by kindness of another lonely soul. Doubt prevailed along with a need to protect him from her world.

"In my time, a handsome scholar would never lack

for lovers or a wife. There must be someone waiting for you to return from your quest."

Clearly, she had an agenda beyond pushing him back into the living. Asking if he was single was so not subtle. Her snakes again flopped in a collective groan. They really wanted lunch, and she might have ruined it. But she was doomed to do so. After all, foolish flirting had gotten her into this cursed mess.

"No one, not for a long time now." He grabbed a brown paper bag and a bottle and walked toward the balcony.

Medusa slumped onto the floor, resting her forehead against a stony reminder of her curse. He was single but young compared to her. She could barely remember the last time she'd flirted with anyone. Not that she had been particularly good, and judging by the embarrassed heat burning into her cheeks, she might be excelling at sounding like a pathetic romantic gorgon instead of the fierce and powerful creature he expected.

He settled down on the floor by one of the outer columns, facing the ocean. "I'm not good at the whole romance thing." His voice carried back into the temple. "I've been dedicated to my work with little room for the useless fluff like flowers, constant texting, phone calls, and the whole discussing your feelings."

A violent crumpling of paper was followed by his muttering. "Apparently, vacation at an archaeological dig and research at archives together isn't spending real couple's time."

Medusa smiled and ran her fingers over the scaly ridges of the serpentine belt of her dress. Everything he described sounded appealing to her. "And your lovers wanted you to fetch flowers for them and pay constant court. Is that what this word texting means?"

He snorted and again made that masculine growling rumble that caused her toes to curl.

"Texting is a rubbish way of stalking someone and demanding you tell them where you are and what you're doing all day. And flowers die. How is that romantic? Rocks don't die. There's nothing wrong with quartz, and rose quartz *is* romantic."

"Rose quartz was Eros' gift to the mortal realms, a symbol of love and passion," she agreed, fluffing her skirts. She imagined a man giving her such a fine gift. Jason might have rough edges, but his heart was in the right place.

"Symbolic gifts don't go over well," he continued. "Apparently, if it had been in jewelry, I might have gotten a pass. It's all just so bloody complicated. Tea with family, group socials, and the whole surprise her with what you're supposed to know she wants, it's all a trap. Courting in the modern world is more like warfare."

"Sounds like Olympus. Only with less blood, curses, and destruction." She giggled when he snorted and grumbled again. Such a man. And one who'd brought her lunch. Clearly, modern mortals were missing out.

She peered around a column at the food he'd laid out and to assess his location. He sat, legs stretched out, back against a column, and facing the ocean. Cautiously, and with no little amount of jittering hand clenching, she ventured toward the basket. When she knelt and sniffed the chicken, her mouth watered. She barely repressed a groan at the salty luscious taste.

"Gods, this is amazing. Tell me more about the outside world. What about your family? You said you lost your parents, but I saw a picture in your bag—" She nearly choked on the admission. "You did leave it behind, the bag I mean." Lame excuse and probably not her best move to admit she'd gone through his belongings. One of her snakes stole a bite of chicken, nearly taking off her finger. She quickly shared the bounty until they calmed and coiled happily in her hair.

"Just my brother and his kids."

The way he gruffly acknowledged his sibling gave her pause even as she tore a hunk of bread from the loaf.

"He and I don't get on. And that's putting it mildly. We're different and always have been. The only thing that kept us talking was my parents. And they've been gone twenty-three years. Probably at the hands of Olympus."

Family issues and Olympians mucking about with her life, she understood all too well. Definitely time for wine, which she swirled around her tongue and sighed. Not as good as the old days, but that was so long ago. Still better than the watered-down tribute left for Athena. She enjoyed another few bites of chicken with goat cheese, intending on asking more.

"Tell me about these five mortal realms," he said.

"If you promise to tell me why you think Olympians murdered your parents."

"Deal."

Discussing all this with mortals was forbidden. Already cursed, miserable, and bored, she saw no reason to hold back. After a few cups of wine, she might as well tempt the proverbial fires of Tartarus.

"There are five mortal realms, Olympus, and the domain of Hades. We're in Earth Realm where your people abandoned old gods in place of new ones, tossing them aside like so much refuse. Of course, the gods still exist, resentful about the betrayal and waiting for your people to figure out what they lost."

"Exactly!" His voice echoed with a palpable excitement. "My department head accused me of losing objectivity and dabbling in mysticism and fringe conspiracies. He was so boxed into preconceived theology and unable to make one original thought. The archaeological evidence combined with scientifically unexplained phenomena supported my theory."

His voice lifted in exuberance, banishing the otherwise morbid essence permeating the dilapidated temple. Medusa lounged on the picnic blanket, enjoying his ramble. His passion for discovery made him even more attractive than his already appealing esthetics. Maybe the wine made her relaxed enough to admit her attraction, but that clean-shaven jaw and firm lips presently engaged in a delightful rant against mortals made her yearn to kiss him. Another dream left to the shadows of night.

"And they ridiculed and dismissed me!" he continued his diatribe. "Those pompous academic types never once said *what if* or questioned odd weather events or written accounts of innovations resulting in bountiful crops when there shouldn't have been. Or incredible architectural advances. And they blacklisted me, calling me a nutter, making sure no one would hire mad Dr. Walker."

"You're not mad." Defensiveness or maybe a protectiveness unfurled until her snakes writhed, matching her mood. "Well, maybe a little because you're having lunch with a gorgon who could end your life with one accidental glance," she tacked on, swirling wine in the plastic cup.

"Maybe I am," he admitted with a drawn-out sigh. "Or mad enough to follow destiny to uncover the truth. Even if it leads to my end. Dying like this would mean something. Especially if I could spend eternity—"

He muttered so softly she didn't quite catch what he said. Maybe she didn't want to know. Food was easier than understanding his complicated motivations or, she hazarded to hope, feelings.

Instead, she reached into the woven basket and pulled out an odd clear crinkling bag with almonds inside. She ripped it open with her teeth and moaned at the crunchy salty treat.

"Jason," she said around a mouthful. "Please don't die here." She washed them down with wine as her stomach burned with worry for him when he didn't respond. "I meant what I said yesterday. No matter how trying you think your life is, there's always something better than here."

"Tell me about the other mortal realms."

Diversionary tactics were something Medusa had observed in warriors attempting to vanquish her. She had used a similar emotional tactic when she received the odd social visit from Hermes or that one time Apollo showed up. Always when they wanted a favor.

"There's Terra," she said slowly between bites and thought on how much to tell him. "It's like Earth Realm only simpler, and the mortals there still worship the Olympian gods. Then there's Atlantia, Lorreum, and the Unspoken."

"The Unspoken? That sounds a bit ominous."

"No one goes there. Zeus forbade it after several of the Olympians never returned, not even to the Underworld. It's used as a threat, the worst punishment

Zeus could hand out."

"Not too far off the legends, then," he acknowledged. "And you're from Olympus?"

"No, I was born on Terra. My parents are Phorcys and Ceto, sea deities. Although I was born different than them or my great sisters. I had few talents and certainly nothing like now. I fit into the mortal world and would run errands for them. It was a simpler life and one I wasted." She swirled her wine in the odd cup that felt so fragile in her hands. Like Jason. "You might like Terra, but you'd never survive, not as you are."

"'Cause I didn't rampage in here with a sword?"

He had a teasing lilt to his voice, more relaxed now. Warmth lapped through her at the growing intimacy between them.

"Something like that."

"My manhood has been called out." He sputtered and cleared his throat. "I'll have you know I've spent weeks camped on several digs, wheeled barrels of rubble. I made the campfire, foraged and fished on my own, and for the useless students who couldn't survive without blogging on social media. I might prefer the company of your kind, listen to their stories, and be a hermit or a scribe passing down knowledge. Might get more respect that way."

"You'd make a wonderful scribe. If you weren't eaten first or taken as a slave."

"I might not do well at the slavery thing. I tend to have opinions."

"And what's your opinion on gorgons?" She poured more wine, almost finishing the bottle. Fishing for compliments wasn't something she was good at, but wine and a nice meal lulled her into a romantic mood without all the death and doom she normally used as a shield.

"I'm fond of the one who didn't kill me right away. Kind of like where she lives, dust and death notwithstanding. She has a wicked sense of humor, and who wouldn't want to spend time talking to a woman who knows the truth about humanity, our history, and how it all went down two thousand years ago?"

"Two thousand!" She glared up at Athena's statue. "I've been on the murder run for far longer than I thought."

"Medusa love, humanity has killed way more than you have. You missed a few wars. And trust me, society would disappoint you with everyone obsessed with money, power, who has a posh flat or expensive car. I think the Olympians must enjoy the misery and greed festering on this world. Maybe they even helped it along."

"They would enjoy your suffering as much as your arts," she admitted, resentment reigniting with the fury of loudly hissing snakes. She knew very well the pettiness and selfish pleasure of Olympians. Medusa wasn't so different as she looked around at stone reminders. Part of her took pleasure in ending them, these ignorant mortals who so easily threw away their freedom. "Jason, I think you need to leave."

"The more you toss me out, the more I want to come back. I'm stubborn that way."

Tears burned at her eyes. She needed to vent and couldn't with him there. He might see her, and then everything would be ruined. Like her whole life. She hunched over, slapping her palms against the gritty stone floor, fighting back the need to lash out.

"I hear chocolate helps. It can soften the rough edges. Like a shot of whiskey and reading about Odysseus."

She lifted her head, releasing a deep breath at his attempt to calm her. She eyed a rat that squeaked before turning to stone. It helped in a vindictive gorgon way.

"Odysseus was an idiot." Her commentary earned Jason's laughter. "Mortals shouldn't lavish praise on alleged heroes who constantly needed godly assistance."

"Now, there's something we both can agree on."

She should be wondering about this special ability he had to both calm and cause her to smile. Instead, she reached for a silver-wrapped package lying amidst lunch that caught the light. She ripped it open and immediately sighed at the sweet, fruity cocoa scent. The silky sweet chocolate melted on her tongue, and she curled up next to the basket. Even her snakes settled into a relaxed mass curling around her neck and ears.

"Jason, thank you for staying. You shouldn't, and you might be an idiot too but a noble one. Most of the noble ones die, you know."

"It does tend to end that way in many of the old stories. Not the worst end given a choice."

He again spoke with a teasing lightness even about such a grim subject.

Her eyes teared with emotion at how much he'd changed her life for the better. Even a dingy temple swirling with the dust of the dead couldn't diminish how he'd broken the cycle of vendetta and death she'd lived for two thousand years.

"I don't want your life to end. You matter to me more than anyone has, maybe ever." She slapped a hand over her mouth too late. The sky darkened and rumbled with thunder. The inevitable uncomfortable silence stretched despite the marble temple vibrating from the building storm.

Jason had said he didn't talk about emotions, and what had she done but crossed another line. She pressed her fingers into her shut eyes, once admired by many, now the means of death. Perhaps the death of her own meager chance at happiness.

"You mean more to me too," he answered slowly but with impact. "I know I buggered into your temple with more attitude than brains. Talking to you made me realize everything I read and thought I knew was wrong. I don't have to see you to know you're no monster. You're better than most of humanity, and you deserve to be heard. I would spend the rest of my life just listening to you talk about how you see things and what you think of the world. I can't say that about anyone else. I mean, it's been nice to have a picnic, talk, and just be in the moment. Feel free to tell me to sod off. Not exactly good at this talking thing."

More tears blurred her vision until they spilled onto the floor, sizzling against the stone like acid. She was a creature that brought death. Not worth his affection or admiration.

"You're doing very well. But I don't believe your world is so terrible that you think me, the most horrible monster imaginable, is better than all the mortals in your world."

"Maybe to you they wouldn't be. Perspective and all that."

He had so vanquished her. Not just her curse, but her heart and herself as a person. Respecting her opinion, offering kindness and conversation along with a nice lunch was what all the others before him had missed. Well, she bit her lip, stifling a chuckle. He was a bit pretty too.

"Thank you for lunch. May I give you a gift in return?"

"You already gave me my life and friendship. I'm only sorry I can't do more for you, take you out for a proper dinner."

"Careful, I might think this was a first date. Before you know it, there may be flowers and more talking about feelings."

He let loose a loud laugh that echoed in the temple. "Love, you deserve all the flowers."

Her face heated at his endearment, and again a giddiness bubbled from a place she'd locked away. So unaccustomed to compliments, she lounged by the basket, tracing the weave, wondering how she could make this day last.

"I found your sketches," she quickly confessed. "I'm leaving them by the basket with a few additions, things I remember from the past and what I know about myself," she added softly, quickly rising and darting behind a statue to pick up his sketchbook, which she propped next to the basket before grabbing a few treats for later. She'd learned to never expect the good things to last. A rumble of thunder seemed to emphasize how fleeting her time with Jason was.

"There's a storm coming, and you should leave while you can. Even Charon has his limits." She was a little wobbly on her feet from all the wine. Even her snakes were hissing and flopping all over her head. The temple spun, and she giggled at herself even as another boom shook the marble.

"I could stay if you want."

Oh, did she want. But there was a difference between want and what must be. His safety came first, and she couldn't trust herself not curl up next to him while he slept. Especially drunken giddy her.

"No, I think it's best for you to rest in a warm bed. But you…you could come back tomorrow if you'd like. Maybe I'll have some more things for your research." She might have been grasping at reasons to entice him to return.

"The temple is research enough."

His footsteps neared, and she shrank behind Athena's statue.

"I meant what I said. I could spend my life studying your temple, writing, and sketching this place. You'd probably get tired of me."

"Never." Wine and drunkenness notwithstanding, she spoke with a certainty struck deep in her bones. As certain as she was anything that saw her would die. Morbid thought notwithstanding.

"Guess we'll have to test your tolerance. I'll see if Erik can pack us another lunch. He was pretty impressed I lived. The village is more aware than you'd think. Could be they try to talk people out of finding you. Not that they stopped me. Guess I rubbed them the wrong way."

Medusa stopped short, palm planted against the cold marble of the statue. "You mentioned an innkeeper earlier. Is this Erik? I'm curious how a mortal knows so much about me and still sends you back to face a monster."

"Like I said, he's been around the past decade, fits in with the locals. Valentine's quite a character. Runs the inn and a bar called the Golden Bow."

Medusa dug her sharpened black nails into the marble until powder coated her fingers. Erik Valentine and the Golden Bow. Olympians had a twisted sense of humor, and if this was who she thought, she'd be spending the next century plotting retribution no matter who she had to bribe.

Chapter Five

After Jason left, the wind swirled dust through the temple until the salty damp from the sea thickened the air. Medusa sat near a tarnished brazier, flames flickering against the shadows. She tucked Jason's hooded shirt between her shoulder and cheek, seeking comfort against the emptiness surrounding her.

His presence had chased away the desolation and loneliness of her prison. Except after having his companionship, the sound of his voice lifting her misery, now she felt the chill of her curse even deeper.

Instead of wallowing and counting the hours to the next day when he'd return, she focused on a disturbing detail. Jason had mentioned an innkeeper who had too much knowledge of her. She expected stories, of course. Epic tales passed down throughout time. But this Erik Valentine had given Jason a list of her fallen assassins.

And when Jason spoke his name, she'd felt a tightening in her chest, and then a familiar hint of myrrh swept through the air.

"Golden Bow my cursed ass." Even her snakes slithered in agitation, clearly feeling the same godly vibe Medusa had. Only a few Olympians would be bored enough to interfere and taunt her. And from how her skin now prickled, one of those Olympians had just invaded her temple.

"This place could use some poshing up."

A masculine voice with an accent not far off Jason's cut through the interminable silence of her home. A very familiar voice and one she hadn't heard in two thousand years and grated on her nerves.

"What does the lad see in all this dust? Or is it the gorgon who has somehow set aside centuries of vengeance for a hot professor? Seriously, all this fluttering hearts and simmering passion zinging about makes Mum and I look bad."

"Erik Valentine!" She set aside the coveted shirt and stormed forward. A few stone statues toppled, victims of her rage. "Where are you?"

"The name's a bit on the nose, but modern mortals are rather oblivious. Although I'm surprised my latest project hasn't caught on, given his area of study. But then he's a bit distracted, isn't he?" His voice bounced off the stone, seeming to echo in every direction.

"Face me, Eros!" Anger and a knot of betrayal fueled her hunt. Animal instincts she rarely acknowledged surfaced as she stalked the interfering god.

"Now that wouldn't be my best plan, would it? I'm a bit busy to test that curse of yours against my Olympian constitution."

"You think you're so clever, toying with people's lives!" A hint of a hiss entered her voice. A rusty sword beckoned her. The heavy metal felt good in her hand. Especially if he'd influenced Jason or worse… Her heart clenched, and tears burned her eyes at how everything between them might be a lie.

Spilling immortal blood wouldn't heal her broken heart. But it would be start.

"I didn't toy with anyone. Really, must you with the

sword?" He stayed hidden from her view but not for long if she had her way.

"Yes, I must. It's been a long time since I got to hack into something." Her snakes joined in her fury and hurt, hissing and sizzling with her curse. Moonlight filtered in the perimeter, revealing a shadow. A flush of heat raced in her veins.

"I'm flattered," he said with a hint of laughter. "But you've got it all wrong. Here's me on holiday when wham! Love so powerful it nearly knocked me on my arse. Without me lifting a finger or an arrow. Intense immortal love that gave me quite a high. In case you're missing it, that would be you and your Jason."

"You expect me to believe that?" She watched as the shadow vanished, then reappeared at a nearby corner of the temple.

"It's the truth. Honestly, my ego's a bit hurt. You two could've been my greatest triumph. Instead, here's me, getting pointers. It's a bit humbling."

She paused her pursuit but wasn't quite ready to let go of vengeance or her sword. "Are you trying to tell me a gorgon succeeded where the god of love failed?"

"Yes, I bloody am. You charmed the uncharmable. He came to die for his cause. I warned him and put up the standard obstacles. Hell, the whole village did their best to stop him. He's not exactly the annoying tourist type they'd send off to oblivion. Of course, then he returned alive and fell over sloppy drunk, mooning over you in my pub."

Her heart swelled, not with anger at this interfering god, but at the man who proved greater than all Olympus.

"You're saying he—" Her throat thickened and clenched before she could utter that one sacred word. A word she never thought would be said to her.

"Ahhh, you didn't think he loved you."

Maybe she would draw blood at his crowing and glee.

"Mortals can be slow. Him especially. Dull and working all the time. This one rarely enjoyed the pleasures around him. Apparently, he prefers the attentions of those he can't see."

Reality had a way of always stealing everything good. And no matter what Eros said, the truth was set in stone around her. She tossed the sword aside with a satisfying echoing clank.

"Even if he does love me, it's a love that can never be. Does that ease your ego?" Sadness carved away any warmth or hope she might have had. Even her snakes seemed to curl closer and cuddle her head. They'd been surprisingly intuitive for implements of doom. But they were like her, victims of a goddess' petulance.

"Rubbish. Love is what inspires mortals to achieve the impossible."

She heard his footsteps grow closer. Dangerous even for him.

"It's pointless. I tried to tell him, warn him away." She wrapped her arms around herself, heartache almost too much to bear at both wanting Jason and knowing these feelings endangered him.

"Ah yes, the futility of mortals loving ones like us. I know what that's like. Maybe that's why I'm here." His voice seemed to be closer, behind her now.

"You?" She snorted, dropping her arms. She could turn and test her power on him. But fear for Jason stopped her. Aphrodite might take her revenge on him, knowing it would hurt Medusa.

"Despite my cause and calling, I've failed to find what you now have, Medusa. A soulmate, it's called in this mortal realm. It's my job to provide mortals a nudge or path to love, and yet my path's full of weeds. It rambles and meanders, and I'm sodding over it. Then there's you proving the impossible with a mortal. So don't waste this opportunity. You might not get another one."

"We can't. One accident, he sees me, and I'd have to end myself. No night of pleasure is worth ending him." Although she really wanted that night without the death and pain. Warmth flushed from her neck to her toes as she imagined what it would be like to ride her hot scribe.

"He doesn't have to see you. A little creativity can go a long way."

The way his voice drew out the words with that subtle flirty innuendo made her clench her muscles until she felt like one of her stone victims. Olympians didn't do subtle. Over-the-top godly acts, lashing out in vendetta, or pushing mortals to their peril was their way. She was an example of one such act. Despite her desire, she wouldn't allow Jason to fall victim in Eros' sudden need to prove his godliness.

"Don't you dare hurt him. I know how the gods think. Blinding him so you can have some sort of victory dance in Olympus will earn you my vengeance." She hurled words laced with a hissing menace as deadly as her snakes. "Don't think because I'm stuck in this temple I can't make good on a threat. My family still has influence even if we're in different realms. There are those in Olympus who owe me favors and aren't fond of you."

"Easy now, and give me a little credit. Blind him?

Bloody Tartarus, Medusa, you've been on this island too long if you think I'd do that."

"You're an Olympian. And everyone knows what you did to Apollo and how it ended for Daphne."

"Oi! I was in my cups that day, and Apollo is an egotistical, insulting prat. He deserved a lesson. And I did feel bad about the nymph. It's not like I haven't paid the price, indentured to my mother's service and on probation. Trust me, that's no picnic. I've made a vow to do better. I also happen to like this mortal who's fallen for you."

"Be still my gorgon heart. Eros likes a mortal and not just to seduce."

"I feel called out," he said with a roll of laughter. "And maybe you have cause. It's not like I've always made the best decisions. Lately, I've found myself envying mortal love."

Medusa saw him in the moonlight, dressed not dissimilar to Jason. Jeans, untucked shirt, long blond hair bound at his neck. He stood still, gazing at a sky dotted with stars she'd often wished upon. A mournful quality entered his voice in how he spoke of love. It lacked the earlier bubbling laughter and taunting of most Olympians and certainly the god of love.

"Eros, why are you here?"

"You've changed. It's good, you talking more. I'm glad. It wasn't fair, what Athena did." He remained still, his gaze fixed on the ocean crashing against the rocks outside the temple.

"And you're good at avoiding answers." Medusa drew back into the shadows even though curious about his motivations.

"Told you, I was drawn to an impossible love. One

not born of me or my mother, but even more potent. A mortal and a gorgon fell so hard so fast nothing I've done could compare." He swung around a column and preened, moonlight highlighting his dimpled smile. "Of course, if I left it up to the two of you, you'd snuff it out. Like I said, I like this mortal, and I've magnanimously granted him my blessing to help the two of you find everlasting love. Which will be fucking impressive."

"Oh no, you won't. This, I mean Jason and I don't need anything from you."

He let out a hard bark of laughter. Tension tightened into a knot in her shoulders. Even her snakes grew rigid and hissed loudly in her ears. She doubted Eros had any altruistic motives.

"Spreading love and passion is part of my job. Making impossible love come to fruition, it's not just a challenge, but proof I'm not some minor love god who needs supervision."

"Eros." Her voice drew out in an exhausted moan. She needed air and possibly a bottle of wine to deal with Eros on a mission that was less about her and Jason and more about ego. She peered out into the velvet night just as a light streaked across the sky.

In the old days, such things had significance. Like Eros' visit. Exhaustion weighed down her limbs.

"It's your job to help others find love. If you're bored, maybe shoot yourself with one of those golden enchanted arrows."

"I'm immune. Love is my destiny but not one I can influence for myself or dally about while I'm still under the control of my mother."

"Bound in servitude, are you? Not an easy existence," she admitted, although withholding too much sympathy. At least until she uncovered his true motivations.

"Knew you'd understand." He strolled along the ocean-side balcony, moonlight glowing against his skin, revealing the glamour of his godhood. "You want freedom to love. So do I. We could both get what we want. You love, and me redemption and freedom."

"Not if Jason's life is at stake."

"He's already asked for my help, and I'm honor bound to fulfill that promise. And it won't take an arrow. You two are the real deal. With a complicated problem."

"There's no problem," she insisted even as her snakes hissed the word *liar*.

"Come on! Stop being so self-sacrificing. It's boring." His annoyance manifested with self-pitying mutters about gods and stubborn gorgons. "You should thank me for, if I do say so, a most brilliant plan to give everyone a happy ending."

Olympus preserve her from interfering gods with delusions of grandeur.

"Eros, I know you feel like you have to prove something—"

"Bollocks. It's not about proving anything. True love exists, and I'm here to make sure it goes off without a hitch. And if I get a little credit, all the better. It's not like love games with silken bindings aren't enticing or useful."

Medusa bit down hard on her bottom lip at the thought of tying up Jason, naked on her bed. She'd had two thousand years and thousands of erotic poems, limericks, songs, and books to fill her head with so many ideas.

She cleared her throat and did her best to douse

those lusty thoughts.

"Eros, I do not care to hear about your perverse sexcapades on Olympus. This is the temple of Athena, you might recall. And the last time a god of Olympus desecrated her temple with his lust, I paid the price."

"Temple sex and the whole ritual orgies are passé. But this isn't about me. It's about you and Jason and love powerful enough to shake the five mortal realms. I may not have set this in motion, but let's just say you've inspired me."

"Inspired you to what?"

"No worries, my favorite gorgon. I've got this. Get some rest. You may need it." Laughter echoed as he disappeared in a shower of gold dust.

She leaned against a pillar, the cool marble a comfort against her skin, heated with thoughts of a tryst with Jason. Except doubt still chipped away at her mind until she began gnawing on her thumbnail. Jason might not want a tryst with her. If Eros was right, then Jason's love could be more emotional than physical. After all, sex with a gorgon wasn't what most mortals would yearn for. Unless he had some kinks. She looked out at another falling star.

"Please let him have a tiny kink for me."

Chapter Six

Sleep deprived and rubbing at his eyes, Jason trudged down the narrow wooden staircase toward the bar. His inner hermit recoiled at the packed space. His stomach, however, growled for breakfast and caffeine. Sketch pad clamped to his chest like a shield, he skirted the room and grabbed a corner table.

The hum of the crowd at the bar and clank of silverware mixed with the scent of warm bread. He rubbed at his eyes again. Was this the Saturday brunch crowd? Blimey, that meant it'd been a week since he'd first discovered the location of Medusa's Island.

Now he sat not on a mission of discovery, but one of intrigue and a touch of attraction for a woman who captured him in a way few had. So much so, he'd stayed up late, thinking about her and studying the sketches she'd made for him.

A mug and coffee were delivered by a girl in jeans and a T-shirt imprinted with the inn's logo, a golden bow. Her black braids made him think of the sketches Medusa had drawn. He flipped open the sketchbook to study them again. The sketches represented more than art or history. They were a connection between him and Medusa. He donned glasses and traced his finger over charcoal drawings of a young woman with black plaits and large expressive eyes.

He doused his coffee with too much cream and

turned a page, again marveling over her artistic talent. She'd drawn depictions of other gorgons, temples, and a trident-wielding Poseidon half risen from the sea.

An ancient Greek dialect he'd had to research lined another page. He'd spent hours translating and laughed at a cheeky limerick. Propped up against pillows with his laptop next to him, he'd stared into space at a poem about the sorrowful daughter of Phorcys and Ceto, reminiscing about the Hesperides Garden and the honeyed nectar of its blossoms.

"Jason! Hero of the modern world! You went straight up last night without so much as a nod."

Erik Valentine jarred him from his thoughts. The innkeeper plunked down opposite him, looking the same as always, blond hair tied back and a twinkle in his blue eyes. Leaning forward, he reached for the sketchbook.

Jason swallowed strong coffee and slid the book out of his reach. Medusa had asked about Erik, and it hadn't been a casual inquiry. Suddenly, he felt a heavy dose of suspicion for everyone in this town. Medusa's protection was his priority even against nosy innkeepers who had pointed him in the right direction.

"Sorry, long day exploring. Got caught up in another one of those freak storms." He pocketed his reading glasses, giving his companion a hint more scrutiny than he had the prior night.

"Freak storms that pop up after you visit a gorgon who's gone sweet on you. Nasty coincidence, those. Funny how you always make it back, not a scratch on you. Almost like you're blessed."

"I'd be the last person to get blessed."

A wide grin spread across Erik's face as he planted his elbows on the table and leaned in closer. "Could've fooled me. Out-of-your-element professor shows up, asking about legends that are sure to lead to your doom. Ignores the warnings of everyone and swans into danger. Yet here you are alive. Funny, that. It's changed you, though, facing your mortality. I can see it in your eyes."

"Points for the flattery and allusion to divine intervention. Bet it sells drinks." Jason watched Erik over his mug of coffee.

The innkeeper's blond head tilted back in a bark of laughter before his gaze landed over Jason's shoulder. "Well, I do sell drinks. And I see the stories behind those who buy them. Those two for example." He waved his hand at a young couple seated behind Jason. "Still in that first flush of love. All comfortable and as easy as breathing. A heated look, bump of hands, sparks of attraction, lust, a kiss in the rain, and then it's all shagging, breakfast, and before they know it, a routine. Too easy. Which means they haven't found the truth beyond passion. True love has to be won. There's got to be a risk or a challenge to overcome."

Jason wanted to snort in derision. A few days ago, he would have. Since he left London, his job, and sanctimonious brother behind, life might have tested his ego and preconceived notions about history and existence in the modern world. He might deny it, but finding Medusa had changed him. Not that he would confess that to the innkeeper.

"Are you going somewhere with this? I mean, why do you care about them or me?"

Erik burst with a lilting laugh until a few people paused to watch him.

"Jason, you continue to wound my ego. It's bloody refreshing. And I like you for it." Erik waved over a waitress who delivered a basket of pastries. He bit into one of the cinnamon-layered phyllo-dough sweets. "Eat. You'll need it for whatever you're planning." He shoved the basket over.

Jason's stomach rumbled, much to his annoyance. He grabbed a pastry and almost hated to admit how hungry he was. That's what happened when he stupidly obsessed on a research project and ignored things like sleep and food.

"I care," Erik continued around a mouthful of pastry, "because I'm interested in human behavior, and it's part of the job, doling out advice over a little liquid courage. My own love life has been complicated of late, but with you and this lot, I can make a difference."

"I'm not looking for matchmaking." Jason sucked down one more drag of caffeine, grabbed another pastry, and pushed back from the table. "In fact, consider me off the market. Now, I've got things to do. Enjoy your whatever." He gestured around the room, another bite of pastry staunching any other possibly sarcastic remark.

"To another date with the lovely gorgon who everyone is pretending doesn't live on the mysterious disappearing island. And to what end? What's your plan, Jason? How will you make love to a woman who has endured millennia of unpleasantness?"

"Unpleasantness?" Jason's blood pounded in his ears at how Erik dismissed Medusa's torment. He did his best to not hurl a coffee mug at him. "I'm not doing this with you. Or wasting time asking how you know that. My day is my business." He stood, tucking the sketch pad under his arm.

"You had to go and pull attitude." Erik groaned. "Fine, here we go, then. Stop." He appeared before Jason in the blink of an eye, T-shirt and jeans molded to a muscular form.

Stillness slammed through the formerly chatter-filled room, turning everyone in the bar into statues. Not unlike Medusa's temple. Except these were flesh-and-blood people.

Jason's heart pounded as he faced the golden-haired innkeeper wearing an arrogant smirk. He'd thought meeting Medusa prepared him for anything. Yet there he stood like a clueless student in one of his lectures. Idiot him. All the clues had been there, so much so Medusa figured it out. He should have. Especially after how his parents died.

"You're an Olympian, and you've been playing me." Bitterness sharpened his words even as a hint of fear tightened a knot in his neck. And not just for him. He couldn't allow Medusa to suffer further at the hands of another immortal.

"It's astounding how blind you've been." Erik casually strolled among the bar patrons, poking a few here and there, some with forks halfway to their mouths. He eventually collapsed onto a nearby chair and grabbed another pastry, still watching Jason. "Bit amusing, you being all oblivious. So focused on proving your theories you missed what was in front of you. Didn't even consider how a quest for truth turned into something more, a passion. Despite all your faults and the roadblocks, you still managed to find true love. That, my friend, is worthy of some extra attention." He reached for another pastry.

"Who are you really?" Jason didn't dare tear his gaze from Erik or whoever he really was.

"Aren't you supposed to be an expert? What other

god cares about getting you loved and laid?" He licked his fingers and arched a brow until Jason felt a wildly inappropriate heat flush through his body.

"The golden bow." Jason could scarcely believe what he was about say, except he was practically dating a gorgon. "Eros."

He looked at the seemingly mortal man before him, jeans, black T-shirt with the bar's logo. With the muscular physique and twinkling eyes, the whole image, it slammed into his chest. Erik fit what a modern-world god of love would be. "I've lost it. I'm gonna wake up in some nut-job hospital."

"You, my friend, are as sane as any mortal in this realm. That's not saying much, mind you. Now, we're past the formalities. Here's the deal."

Jason collapsed onto the chair, needing more than cold coffee if he was to wrap his brain around this turn in his life. Until a singular thought cut through disbelief. Eros had a reputation. One which he'd named the pub for.

"Did you shoot me or her?" He didn't want to know the answer. In fact, he'd rather plunge into the sea and let it take him the way it took his parents rather than learn the exhilaration and heart-pumping anticipation he'd experienced was a lie.

"Gods, but you two are meant for each other. She asked the same thing, and the answer is no. You two are the real deal. The inspiration that's dragged me out of boredom and the repetition of watching mortals toss away everything I give them."

"But we're not, that is, I'm—" His usual ability to articulate, talk, and argue his way into and out of anything fled. He'd just met Medusa and wouldn't presume to make any romantic declarations that might burden her. For the love of all mankind, he was a scientist, and she was his research. And he was sticking to that excuse.

"Jason, you're the most pig-headed, tunnel-visioned mortal of them all. Always turning away from every chance at love. And yet here you are. On a quest for knowledge but finding so much more, proving the whole bloody pantheon and every realm wrong. Love conquers everything, and I am fucking here for it!"

Speechless, Jason stared at the very much not mortal man who slammed his hand onto the wooden table. Chatter and the clink of glasses and silverware resumed. The waitress, Petra, appeared with her ever-present glare at him before delivering fresh mugs and another picnic basket.

"Anything else?" she asked with a touch of bite in her voice until Eros tilted his head charmingly.

"I've got this, love. No worries, we're on the right track here."

"No, we're not on any track," Jason insisted.

Petra's softened face for Eros turned into a hastily exhaled sigh. She muttered a few curses in Greek before she left them.

"You've got it wrong." Jason made another pathetic attempt at denial that even he knew sounded lame.

"I'm never wrong about this. Love is real. Stop questioning and accept it. As well as my favor and blessings doled out for reminding me unlikely love is still possible. Even if you lot don't worship me. Which you should, given all my work." He eyed an older couple leaning in close, eyes crinkled with more than joy. Their hands were clasped, rings evident of their commitment.

Jason was reminded of his parents. Their love had never wavered. But he wouldn't allow that to sway him into giving any immortal control over his life. "You tried to talk me out of going to find her. Why do that if you were so sure she and I would be a thing?"

"Questioning a god will get you nowhere. Trust me, mate. We're good at enigma, and our moods shift on the slightest whim. Best take what I'm giving you, which is a chance to love her. To do that, you've got to problem solve."

A black silk scarf dropped on Jason's head. Cool silk slid down his face until he caught the fabric and held it up in between him and Eros.

"Anyone who gazes at Medusa turns to stone. Even a reflection can do the trick, especially to her. You've already figured out you don't need to see her to fall in love. Sometimes the greatest pleasures come from denying one sense to amplify others."

Damned if his libido didn't burn hot at the cool silk sliding through his fingers. Or how Eros might be laying on the whole lusty-god aura.

But then his thoughts turned straight to Medusa and the one thing he might have mused in the darkness of the night, but at the same time he chided himself about. Wondering what her skin felt like, how he might like to worship each and every delicious curve of the woman behind the myth. And the blindfold could make that fantasy a reality.

"I thought about a blindfold last night." He slid the fabric through his fingers and held it up to the light.

"Course you did. But not like this. Light blocking. Woven by Clotho herself," Eros said with glee and a prideful boast.

"And that's not frightening, given her reputation. Tell me again why you'd do this for me? What's in it for you?"

Eros groaned and tipped back in the wooden chair. He leaned so far it should have fallen until he slammed forward. Jason flinched back from the clearly annoyed blond god.

"One more demand and the whole thing is off. I can take it away as fast as I offered it."

Jason hated to admit how much power Eros held over him in that moment. It scalded and burned in his belly more than whatever alcohol he'd been given the other night.

"All right," he grudgingly admitted and quickly wrapped the scarf in his hand. "In the big scheme of things, what does this cost? I can't let her be hurt. I care—" He swallowed the words back. They seemed too important to say there. And after all, in the old tales, words had power, and he wasn't keen on giving Eros any more over him.

"Save the words for your lover. But you're right. True love comes with a price. I can't tell you what that'll be. But I know someone who can. Not that you're ready for that. First you need to get out of here and go feed your lovely lady. No doubt she's pacing a hole in that temple, waiting on you."

Jason wasn't sure how much of what Eros said to believe. The historian in him, the one who catalogued mythologies and accounts of the Greek pantheon, wanted to dig deeper. But the part of him ready to leave research behind itched to escape back to Medusa.

"Go on, get out of here before I change my mind," Eros taunted, pushing off the table, essentially ending the conversation.

Given the narrowed glare directed at him, Jason quickly grabbed the basket the waitress, Petra, dropped on the table, and got the hell out of the bar. But not before he did a test run.

Back in his room, he wrapped the blindfold around his eyes. After crashing into a couple of walls, which resulted in a lump on his forehead, he felt confident a new realm of possibilities awaited him with Medusa.

A quick peek into the basket proved only lunch and no other surprises awaited him. Satisfied with his new plan, he slipped on his coat and didn't stop for any more chitchat as he raced through the bar toward his scooter. His only side trip was to buy art supplies, flowers, and chocolates. The irony did not escape him. His scowling former self would have flinched at the thought. But this was Medusa, and she wasn't like any other woman.

The sun beat down as he made the winding trip up the hill to the secret path. Sweat beaded on his neck in the unusually nice weather. Stowing his scooter, he stopped for a moment, thinking on what Eros had said.

Romantic love had always been conceptual to him. A thing others did and wrote about. A simple cocktail of hormones and urges to find companionship. He'd tried it and found the whole thing more work than it was worth. Until he'd met Medusa.

Eros had called them impossible lovers. Something about that phrase swelled more than his heart. A base instinct he would never inflict upon a woman who had been so taken advantage of. A woman he admired, and...oh, who was he kidding? Part of him wanted to touch her, gently, reverently, and maybe passionately. Blimey, he wanted to know what it felt like to hold someone who captivated him and gave him a jolt of happiness like proving a theory in an old tome everyone else dismissed as drabble.

He eyed the blindfold and tied it around his neck. It had to be her choice, and if it wasn't, he could take a dip in the sea and, well, pretend he wasn't a hormone-driven mortal. On that less-than-noble thought, he clambered down the steep path, working off some of those annoying hormones.

When he made it to the beach, the sea breeze kicked up the blue-green waters of the Aegean against the rocky shore, chilling his sweat-slicked skin. He stepped onto the rickety dock and rang the old tarnished bell. On schedule, the sky turned gray, and the clouds seemed to sink down, turning the water a murky blue.

"You again." The cranky ferryman's gruff voice emerged from the thick mist rolling toward shore. The rhythmic splash as he paddled the skiff was now a welcome sound. "Maybe this will be the day, eh? I'll finally give Hades a decent heroic soul from this realm."

"Don't know about decent. But might be your day, though, not for the reasons you're thinking. Here." Jason shoved a white paper bag of toffee chews and orange fizz at him and climbed aboard.

"Bribery won't keep your soul from Lord Hades' realm."

Apparently, it did buy Jason passage. And with the ferryman's bony mouth full of toffee, it passed quietly. Even the sea seemed less chaotic, delivering him to the island without the typical roiling and tossing about. He didn't waste time once they nudged the dock, taking the gravel path with ease.

"Medusa, love!" He called her name with every

ounce of affection he had in him. Something new considering his usual greeting when meeting up with anyone was an announcement of takeout or why he was late.

"Jason."

He didn't miss the sigh in her voice.

"I brought us a meal and a few other things. Hope you like violets." He paused at the main entrance, giving her time to settle herself. He refused to act the part of bullying invader storming her home. He'd also rather live long enough to try the blindfold.

"Did you have a restful night?" she asked.

"I stayed up admiring your art. Afraid I may have overslept this morning." He made his way into the darkened temple, weaving his way around the stone remnants of those who'd attacked her.

He barely glanced at them, no longer curious. One deep breath of the cool, damp atmosphere and the tension from breakfast with Eros fled. The ocean crashing outside felt more welcoming than the sun-warmed island he'd left.

He stopped at Athena's statue dominating the temple. The blanket from their prior picnic was spread out, and Medusa had placed clay bowls, goblets, and a pitcher painted with art that looked fresh, vibrant, and something he would have studied for hours.

The pottery and artwork drove home how unique these visits were. And the significance of his conversation with Eros. Should he tell her about Eros? He rolled that around in his mind as he focused on the present.

"I loved your art," he said as he knelt on the blanket. "I brought you a sketch pad, charcoals, and some pastels."

"Careful, you might give a girl ideas."

"The violets didn't give me away?" he flirted back at her teasing and set said bouquet in one of the cups he filled with water. "I enjoyed the poetry as well. I love a wicked pun."

"Maybe I enjoy a wicked scribe with a taste for musty temples."

"It's not the temple I'm here for." He unpacked the basket filled with another robust feast with wine, stuffed grape leaves, lamb kebabs, tarts, and truffles. Eros didn't play around. Jason didn't want to either.

"There's something I have to tell you." He decided to get the whole Eros part out of the way. He might not be the most romantic bloke, but he'd learned a rather painful lesson from one girlfriend that not telling her he'd had a drink with her cousin ended in a tirade and tea being hurled. Then he had that stubborn compulsion to ask Medusa her opinion.

He spent a moment tossing his coat aside and then unwrapping crusty tarts, thinking exactly how to explain his morning chat with Eros. The god had mentioned a visit to Medusa, so it wasn't like she didn't already know Eros was around.

It was the slight hitch in her voice as she said *Jason*, followed by a heavy silence, that made him realize he'd waited a minute too long to explain.

"You have to go home, and I…won't. I won't see you again." She quickly finished with an anguish in her voice that struck him like one of the rusty swords scattered about her temple.

The assumption he'd leave combined with her shaking broken voice punched him in the gut.

"No, what… No!" He stopped and unknotted the scarf until it lay in a pool of black in front of him. "I'm not going anywhere, and even if I did, I don't have a home to return to. You're stuck with me. Which I gather is the reason I received a lecture from the god of love himself."

"Eros." She spit the name out with such venom followed by loud thuds as if several of her stone invaders had been turned to dust.

That did not bode well for a romantic day.

Chapter Seven

Fiery rage coursed through Medusa's veins. Eros, that meddling, drama-seeking thorn in the backside of all Olympus, toyed with her Jason. If he did anything to him... Her snakes whipped around her head until nearby stone monuments exploded into dust and shards. Clenching her hands, she stormed around her hidden alcove, hurling broken pottery at a wall inscribed with blessings to Athena. Probably a mistake.

"You know, I understand the raging—" Jason's distant voice interrupted her tirade. "Did a little of that when my parents died. Eros isn't worth ruining a day I'd like to spend with you."

"You can't trust him. No matter what he promised."

Eros had offered up quite the temptation to her. The thought of trusting him even a little chafed like the incessant damp dreariness of her temple.

"I don't trust him." Jason's footsteps echoed, followed by the dull thud of wine being uncorked. "He's an Olympian, and they're a capricious lot. He admitted he has a certain reputation and that as much as he wanted credit, he didn't hurl any arrows our way. In fact, he seemed a bit keen on us, that we have something special growing between us. Quite a compliment from someone like him."

Once again, Jason vanquished her rage, turning her into a sputtering pool of romantic girl wanting flowers.

Which, when she peeked out of her alcove, he'd brought her.

"Your visits are more precious than the finest Olympian ambrosia," she tentatively admitted, and her stomach clenched in anxiety. He hadn't elaborated on what special meant. Was she too effusive in her affection? She chewed on her bottom lip, overthinking things like emotions and how not to chase off a suitor.

"This is the part where I should say something romantic." He heaved a huge sigh and tipped his head back, exposing the thick muscular neck she'd dreamed about.

She ducked back into the shadows, nervously tugging at her gown, trying not to think of how she'd like to show him how romantic he was. Especially if he took off his shirt. Gods, but she needed to scrub her clearly sex-obsessed mind and focus on things like daily groveling to Athena.

"Truth is I can lecture at length and publish papers about the cultural impact of the Hellenistic gods, but grand romantic declarations get all muddled. All I know is that the last two days have been the best of my life. I'm not ready to walk away from whatever this is between us."

Honesty laid out before her, Medusa couldn't walk away from him now. Even if a lightning bolt shattered her temple. Eyeing the roof nervously, she succumbed to the heady combination of him and her own yearning. The reward when she peeked past curtains was enough to leave her gasping and bunching the worn fabric in fingers that could be doing so much more. He lounged next to another basket, T-shirt stretched across his broad shoulders as he ate grapes like Dionysus. Except blindfolded.

Gods help her. Suddenly, her temple seemed warmer and less dreary. The scent of roasted lamb wafted toward her, but even more potent was hot male essence. Tanned from the sun, he smelled like sea spray and cedar, even from a distance.

Going to him would be so easy. But years of misery and the repercussions of her last tryst left her as still as one of her victims.

"This won't work." No three words had hurt more. One of her snakes even thumped her on the temple with a hiss that sounded suspiciously like—*fooollisshhh. Get treaatttss.*

She hated rejecting what was a very romantic gesture and one of trust. "But thank you for trying. It's the most romantic thing anyone has ever done for me."

"I wish I could take credit. It was Eros who provided the whole godly blessed guarantee I won't see anything through this bit of silk. And don't think I didn't test it. I promise you I can't see anything and have the contusion to prove it." He rubbed a spot on his forehead. "It's why I didn't wear it into the temple. I'd probably trip and break my neck, and that would be a rubbish way to die."

A smile broke through tension's vice-like grip at his teasing tone. Along with a need to kiss the raised bump and make it better. Well, among other things she'd like to kiss. She ran her fingers across her warm cheeks, imagining him cupping her face, touching her like she hadn't been in two thousand years. Yet worry slithered in the back of her mind, stealing thoughts of tasting his lips or brushing soft kisses along his jaw.

"The power of my curse is nothing compared to one strip of cloth. Even one blessed by Eros."

"Eros said it's made by Clotho. I gather that trumps your curse."

Worry turned into a knot of suspicion. "The Fates don't give gifts out of charity." Now commenced her nervous pacing and thoughts about the powers at work, powers that didn't do favors and enjoyed torment. "Eros is notorious for his affairs. He could have romanced her for a favor. That would be so typical. And dangerous if he spurned her."

Medusa nervously traced the cool metal of her serpentine gold belt. She'd never met Clotho or any of the Fates. Was this their way of snipping Jason's life to make Eros look bad?

"I knew the risk. And Eros, he was a bit touchy on the whys and cost. It's why I tested it. Besides, Eros doing this has to benefit him somehow. So please have lunch with me. I swear to you I can't see anything." He reached for the basket, feeling around until he pulled out a wrapped package.

She really shouldn't. But he looked so hopeful, and he'd laid out a delicious lunch, and he looked rather delicious himself.

"Promise me you'll shut your eyes too. And make sure it's well knotted." She bit her lip nervously but still thrilled at the prospect of sitting close to him.

"Triple tied and my eyes are shut. It'd be a shame if I fell asleep."

The cajoling rumble in his voice broke her resolve. Even though he couldn't see her, she was compelled to straighten her plain white gown. She quickly found a jar with rose oil and dabbed it behind her ears and between her breasts. Her snakes hissed complaints.

"Suck it up. You've had thousands of years to do as

you please. Remember, he brought us lunch again. Be nice." She tangled her fingers in her snakes and ebony plaits, combing through them until both settled around her shoulders. He would never see her, so looks didn't matter. Yet she still remembered when they had.

She pushed aside the weathered and stained white curtains enshrouding her tiny sanctuary. Wary and skittish, she took her time. Trailing her fingers across the cold, rough stone of her adversaries, she watched him fumble, cursing softly as he pulled more items out of the basket.

Once again, happiness flushed through her limbs until she felt light enough to float. Well, except the not-so-pure part that wanted to tear loose the band holding back his hair and show him exactly how close she'd like to be with him.

She eventually lowered down until she knelt behind where he lounged, tempted to wrap herself around him, rubbing her cheek against his shoulder. Instead, she nervously twisted a fold in her gown around her fingers. "Don't turn toward me, please."

"As milady commands."

She bit down on her lip. His voice and how he tilted his head, exposing a stretch of neck, leveled up the fluttering in her chest to outright drooling desire. The spectacular view of his jean-encased ass caused her to sigh and imagine the possibilities. She had to use serious willpower not to touch. Clearing her throat, she focused on something safer, like pouring wine.

"Tell me what Eros said to you that made you think he's getting something out of helping you." She leaned over him, reaching for the wine bottle. She might have enjoyed brushing his firm shoulder and inhaling his woodsy clean scent. Pouring wine and focusing on Eros seemed a good distraction.

"He said he was drawn to what was happening between us. Was envious, and I got a feeling he wanted some glory helping a mortal and gorgon have a nice…date."

She nearly spilled the wine at how he paused and confirmed their courtship. She set a goblet down next to his hand and did what she'd yearned to do and laid her hand on his.

Warm, he was so warm to the touch, and tingles shot up her arm. He drew his thumb across her knuckles. She needed to breathe, except touching another life without her curse getting in the way brought tears to her eyes.

Overwhelmed, she yanked her hand away. "I'm sorry, I shouldn't have—"

"Course you should. It's our second date. Bet our friend Eros is even having a party for us. Although he might have more than hand-holding in mind."

Rolling laughter shook her, and a dizzying happiness blossomed until her temple no longer seemed dismal but brighter. "I'm sure he does. But you don't have to. Unless you want." She trailed off suggestively and then had a moment of soul-crushing anxiety.

"Maybe I do want."

Fires of Tartarus, he flirted back. Oh, she was out of practice in this flirting thing. His stomach made a growling noise, giving her a momentary reprieve. Then she let loose a snorting laugh, breaking the tension.

"Sorry, didn't have much breakfast this morning. Was in a bit of a rush. That's not meant as commentary on where we were heading with this."

"I like a man with an appetite." She might be better

at this flirting thing than she'd thought.

"A woman after my own heart." Jason grinned until his cheek dimpled.

From that moment, an ease settled around them. She lounged closer to his head, seeking intimacy as they both enjoyed lunch. Enjoyment might be an understatement at the sensual pleasure of watching him slip morsels between his lips. Each delicious bite added to the seduction of his presence. Even her snakes hissed a sigh at the spicy lamb. Medusa wasn't far behind, groaning at each of the salty, herb-soaked morsels. But that sumptuous warmth wasn't just from the lamb.

"So Eros paid you a visit too. Did you let him have it?" Jason asked, bumping his hand against hers as he drank wine and reached for the plate filled with stuffed grape leaves.

"He ran from me."

Deep, growling, masculine laughter rolled through her temple again, chasing away the doom that hung in the air. "Brilliant! Don't ever let that Olympian lot make you feel less than the powerful woman you are," he said, still chuckling and fumbling for a kebab.

Medusa's face flushed hot. Her snakes even seemed to preen under his praise. Jason had a way of seeing things she'd been too blinded by guilt and bitterness to see. And no matter how much it might hurt later, she loved him for that and for every ramble and oblivious-to-danger visit he made to her temple.

On a wave of affection, she reached for the elusive kebab he had been unable to pluck from the skewer. She held the morsel to his mouth. When his fingers wrapped around her wrist, a silky liquid fire raced through her until her toes curled. The first brush of his lips left her craving to taste him.

He slid his thumb across her pulse point, and she nearly spontaneously combusted. What an end that would make to the feared gorgon. Killed by unrequited lust.

"Medusa."

Her stomach swooped at the way he groaned her name. Heat rushed through her, banishing logic, survival instincts, and that tiny voice that screamed she was making a mistake.

She brushed her lips against his, just tasting a hint of their meal. Nothing had prepared her for a man who wasn't in a hurry. She tilted her head, reveling in the slow languid slide of his lips. He rested a hand on her hip as she sank closer to him.

The world faded until she was aware of nothing but his warmth, kissing, and the delightful tugging at her bottom lip until the first swipe of his tongue coaxed a moan from deep in her chest. Lust fueled her need to feel his hard body against hers. Gods, she wanted to rip his shirt off.

One tiny annoying thing she hadn't anticipated. Her snakes curiously slithered forward, tongues flicking and surrounding their joined faces.

She jerked back. "I'm sorry. I…I didn't mean…"

"I did," he said with a lilting voice filled with amusement, not quite facing her but not turned away either.

"Aren't you repulsed?"

"Well, the snakes are part of you, and other than a little tickle, I was more preoccupied by the woman snogging me."

"I want to believe that. Believe us being together

like this is possible." Fear dampened lust. She couldn't bear him turning away from her in revulsion.

"You know, I've always liked snakes."

Laughter burst out at how crazy he sounded. "My curse is more than a garden snake," she finally said once she caught her breath.

"They're part of you," he repeated and sat up, still not quite facing her.

He reached out a hand, which Medusa took, pressing his palm to her cheek.

"It's okay to touch me," he assured. "I know you've been alone for a long time. We can take it as slow as you want. But you shouldn't be afraid. When I touch you, I feel soft skin, a flesh-and-blood woman, not a myth or someone to fear. The blindfold is such a gift. Makes every other sense more alive. I want to indulge in all those senses and other kinds of interesting touching."

Her chest flushed at how he cupped her face, his thumb tracing her lips. She imagined how his eyes would darken in passion.

"I like interesting. And touching." She pressed her lips into his palm.

Another miracle was gifted when her snakes didn't just explore but accepted him, flicking their tongues at his wrist until curling back on her head.

"Show me." His rough voice left no questions.

Every sex fantasy poured out as she captured his lips, shoving him down. Her gown hitched up as she straddled his hips. His arms banded around her middle, strong and manly. A groan vibrated in her chest. Centuries of loneliness were vanquished with a swirl of his tongue against hers.

She broke away only long enough to pull her gown

over her head before diving for his mouth, pinning him down. He let loose a groan and laugh. The bulge in his jeans made her grind down, ready to ride him hard.

"Lie still." Apparently, aggressive love play was her new go-to.

"I want to feel you." His hands rested on her bare hips, fingers digging into her flesh each time she rutted against him.

She shuddered at how the metal teeth of his trousers' fastening sent delicious tingles against her feminine heat. "Stretch out your arms."

"Your wish is my command, but if you keep doing—" His hips bucked. "Bloody hell, this isn't going to last long."

"It's not the time. It's the skill." She slid his shirt off past his blindfold, revealing the hard planes of his chest and a fascinating tattoo. "*Aletheia*. Truth." She traced the black lines of the ancient Greek word in the middle of his chest.

"More like too much tequila after a shoddy peer review and a call from my brother," he gruffly confessed before his expression softened. "Maybe it was a sign or self-fulfilling prophecy drawing me here."

She leaned forward, trailing kisses across his jaw. "I think it was just you."

"I—"

She cut off any denial when she raked her nails down his chest, her breath catching as she felt his heart hammering and heat rolling off him. She ached to lick her way across his body, tracing his nipples and following the trail of hair tapering down to his waist.

The metal fastening on his trousers intrigued her, and she flicked the connected tab.

"I…do you need me to—"

"No, I'm enjoying this. Mortals are so very clever with their modern technology and layers of unnecessary clothing."

"Right now, I'm gonna agree it's all bleeding unnecessary."

She lowered the metal tab, the strange metallic teeth parting to reveal straining blue cotton underclothing.

She pressed her hand against his bulging hardness, her toes curling at the solid palmful of manhood. The anticipation was shared based on how he arched beneath her and clamped his hands onto hips.

"This would work better if I got these off."

The guttural groan in his voice caused liquid heat to pool exactly where she wanted him to be. Slow no longer appealed. She toyed with the waistband of his jeans before sliding to the side to help remove the obstacle to her satisfaction. He eagerly lifted up and shimmied his hips. He sat up to finish removing his jeans only to find his boots in the way. With a few tugs, he sent his boots and jeans flying, freeing every bit of flesh she wanted to memorize and claim.

The thud of his shoes and clothing smashing into clay pots was nothing compared to the muscled, thick-waisted man with legs like a gladiator.

"Medusa, love."

She didn't give him a chance to ruin the moment with words, dropping to her knees and straddling him. Her mouth covered his as his arms again banded around her. Cradling him intimately, she ran her fingers over the knot of his blindfold and smiled against his mouth.

Each gentle swirl of his tongue emboldened her to push things further. She shoved him backward, pinning him to the blanket-covered floor. Confidence and passion tightened in her belly, and she reveled in skin-on-skin contact.

His chuckling moans along with how he trailed his fingers down her spine, cupping her ass, dispelled any doubts as to his desire for all of her, gorgon and woman.

Long languid kisses mixed with her grinding her hips against his hardness. Silken heat drenched between her legs until the mere act of rutting almost pulled the trigger of her desire.

After one delicious nip of his lower lip, she pulled back, breathless and needful.

Satisfaction strummed in her body at his reactions, how his body flushed and arched up to meet hers.

"My only regret is not seeing your eyes." Although she certainly enjoyed every other part of him. Including drawing her nails across his abdomen to get a firm grip on his manhood. Power wasn't all about death. Sometimes one wielded it in pleasure. A nice change for her.

"I've seen your self-portraits," he admitted in that low gravelly voice that thrummed inside of her. "I like to think I have a decent imagination of what we might look like together." He slid his hands to her hips, stroking her with his thumbs. "Sorry I don't have any romantic declarations, but—" He gulped a calming breath before shuddering. "Medusa…I'm about to pop off just feeling you."

The way he said her name, voice deep and drawing it out like a blessing. No one had ever spoken her name like he did, and it unleashed a fire in her. She wanted to merge with him, ride him into oblivious and orgasmic pleasure. Maybe that was a dangerous thing. Mortals were so fragile.

"Jason, this… That is to say I haven't done this in a while. I don't want to hurt you." The moment she spoke, an embarrassed regret stilled her. Even her snakes smacked her on the face. Only she could ruin her one chance at sex, even with her hand wrapped around the object of her ultimate satisfaction.

He shook with a deep rolling laugh. "Love, me and my rather impressive manhood would be sadly disappointed if you stopped. I'd rather enjoy shagging ourselves mindless, and I'll take the risk of a broken bone or bruise. In fact, I'd be chuffed to brag how I had the best sex of my life and earned love wounds."

And this was why she loved him. Brave, funny, and wouldn't let anything get in the way of a good time. Not even his neurotic gorgon lover. Lust and her inner dominant sex ego reasserted.

"I wouldn't want to disappoint you or your very impressive manhood." Which she stroked until he gasped and dug his fingers into her hips.

"I won't last long if you keep that up."

Leaning in until her nipples grazed his chest, she darted one more kiss along the prickly stubble of his jaw. She guided him inside her and sat back.

A delicious heat stretched and filled her just as she'd fantasized. She swore the temple shook with the intensity of tingles racing across her sex.

"Jason." She rocked against him, swirling her hips, getting the perfect friction and pressure as he moved with her.

She leaned forward, grabbing his shoulders and grinding and chasing the pounding heat, the cusp of pleasure like a ragged edge just out of her grasp. Thunder rumbled through the temple, but it was nothing like Jason's thrust upward to meet her hunger. Or how he parted his lips, gasping her name.

She licked his neck and then clamped her teeth on the juncture between his neck and shoulder, reveling in what it meant to have all of him, real warm flesh damp and salty with desire. Losing herself in the moment, free from the responsibility of her curse, she immersed herself in pleasure. When his clever fingers slid into her slick heat, teasing her clit, she mewled with the need to satisfy the want fluttering deep in her core.

"Medusa, I'm…I'm almost there, please, love."

"Yes!" She groaned, pressure and heat building in shuddering waves between them.

The strain and pace of their movements quickened. Each time he thrust upward, her body tightened with the buildup of pleasure. She narrowed her focus to feeling until there was no longer a temple or curse. Just Medusa and Jason. He slid one hand to the nape of her neck, and his fingers boldly tangled with her snakes.

An erotic power flared from where her snakes flailed and hissed a song of ecstasy.

Whipping her head back, she ground her hips against him.

On the cusp of satisfaction, her spine tingled, and her pulse thundered in her ears. Liquid heat exploded until, in one more sweet gasping clench of muscles, her cries echoed, and her body spasmed with euphoria. Soon joined by her lover's shouts of completion.

Trembling with a lapping silky sensation, bonelessly, she slid across his body as if she were one of her snakes. "Jason," she whispered against his chest, laying soft kisses up to his face, wishing more than anything they could bask together completely, no mask, no curse, just them.

"That," he said haltingly, drawing circles on the base of her spine, "was the big one, love. I want you to know you're my one. I never thought I'd say that. My mum always said I'd know when I met the right girl. Just never thought it would be the shag of my life."

Love filled this place of death. But then that's part of what he'd done for her. Foolish mortal that he was. She was his and he was hers.

"You are my one too. And I've never been so glad someone came to my temple to so badly slay me. I mean, this is much nicer than swords and arrows."

"Much better."

They snuggled together until drowsiness seeped across her.

"Will you hold me?" she murmured against his neck.

"For the rest of my life if you'll let me."

"In a damp, crumbling temple with awful food and occasional annoying godly visitors."

"We'll order takeaway."

Giggles, which had become a common occurrence for her since she met him, shook through her into him until she felt him relax, and she drifted into a blissful sleep.

Chapter Eight

Jason awakened with a tickle on his neck. He squinted and blinked against the darkness before remembering he had a blindfold on. He reached toward the gentle nudge against his ear and bumped into a cool slinky snake.

Nothing in his life had prepared him for the languid amusement at waking up to his girlfriend's snakes gently flicking their tongues against his finger.

Medusa rolled over, stretching an arm across his chest. When she mumbled in ancient Greek, snuggling into his side, warmth stretched across his torso. Along with a sleepy relaxed ease. A day earlier, seduction and sex hadn't been his plan, and yet there he was, blindfolded and naked in bed with her.

Liar. Fine, he'd thought about it with the blindfold. No sense denying that. His face stretched tight from what he was sure was a stupid had-his-brains-shagged-out grin. Or maybe it was that unbelievable lazy happiness that he'd never quite understood until then. He didn't even care that he had a crick in his back from the cool stone floor seeping through the thin picnic blanket. Or the vigorous lovemaking that had continued into the night, which might have included him on his knees at one point.

"Jason."

Her purring his name combined with the trail of

kisses up his jaw confirmed this was the best way to wake up. Maybe he'd devise a plan to always wake up with her. Without the cold, hard floor.

"Good morning. Or at least I think it is. You'll have to confirm that." He tapped his blindfolded temple.

"It is and the best morning in two thousand years."

He turned his head to find soft pliable lips. Kissing her, the soft flick of her tongue against his as she wrapped him in her arms, felt right and easy. He gently pulled away, tracing a thumb along the curve of her hip. "Yesterday was amazing. You're amazing."

Her answering giggle combined with her fingers tracing what he was sure was a stubbled jaw gave him contentment. He was never one for post sex cuddles or wrap-up, but with her, he wanted to lie in, enjoy the moment.

"Does it bother you, the blindfold? I could go and hide for a while." The tentative and almost shy quality of her voice tugged at feelings he couldn't deny.

"No, don't go. We could have breakfast and talk." He nearly choked.

Feelings, flowers, and now a foreign compulsion for a post-sex chat. His muscles locked at the reality of that *R* word he'd never thought would be back in his vocabulary. Yet there he was, Jason the un-datable, grumpy madman obsessed with legends. He was arse over kettle in love and in a relationship with a gorgon. It didn't frighten him half as much as it should.

Not the gorgon part. He rather found it poetic how his love for his work had manifested into the embodiment of his snake-cursed lover.

An awkward silence stretched as he struggled for the proper lover-y thing to say. It was his idea to talk. Bloody rubbish idea. Her soft laughter and the scrape of her nails as she drew symbols on his chest seemed to give him an out.

"You really don't do this much, do you?" Her husky voice teased him into a response.

"Post-coital love talk is not my strength."

She burst out into loud guffaws echoing around him until he couldn't help but chuckle in response, turning onto his side toward her.

"I should feed you. That's the gentlemanly thing to do after such a vigorous night."

She hummed and nipped at his shoulder. "I liked our vigorous night. You fed me yesterday, so maybe I should be the one offering a meal."

He leaned forward and found her lips tantalizingly close. Of course, kissing was only part of his plan to show her the lengths of his gentlemanly way to thank her, like sliding his hand up the curves of her body. He cupped her breast, gently teasing her nipple. It would be so easy to tell the world to sod off and make love with her all day. Reluctantly, he ended the luxurious snog, heaving a shuddering breath.

"That's my kind of breakfast." His stomach rumbled, and he internally winced. "Sorry, love. Pesky mortal needs like food and the loo prevail."

She hummed, and the weight of her legs entangled with his lifted, leaving a slight chill and loss. Until her firm grip on his arm hoisted him upward to standing. He did love a strong, capable woman.

"Well, I have those needs too. Do you trust me?" She slipped her arm around his and guided him forward.

"Always." Which was damned odd coming from him. Trust was something he didn't give often after years of defending his work. The sigh she gave at his response did something for that masculine pride post shag. Relaxed, he lived in the moment.

Following her lead, he listened to seagulls calling out in the distance and the faint sound of the sea crashing against the rocky shore.

They stopped in an area near trickling water.

"I smell oranges."

"Yes, it was in a basket Hermes delivered yesterday."

"Tribute to Athena?" he asked as she placed his palm on a cool stone wall with water splashing nearby.

"Usually is. But sometimes, she who guards this temple receives gifts from gods, demigods, and those who want me to vanquish someone. I'll leave you to refresh while I gather breakfast." Warms lips brushed his cheek until he thought he'd chuck the whole refresh idea and invite her to share a bath. Which might be in her thoughts as she remained curled against his back.

An epiphany hit him like a chilly gust of wind on his nether regions. He'd taken a dive off the jaded-man-of-the-world-on-a-mission wagon and fallen into the sappy-love wagon. And that was something he'd never expected, and Eros must have been laughing his arse off.

"There are fresh linens to your right. Promise you'll keep the blindfold on," she murmured in a husky voice against his ear.

The nervous catch in her voice struck him in the heart as if Eros had shot him. He hoped he hadn't because he wanted this to be real. "I promise, and honestly, it may never come off."

He swore she smiled against his back before sliding her hand over his shoulder, guiding his hand along damp stone passing through falling water to a corner that carried the scent of the sea with a hint of refuse.

"I won't be long."

How did she make four words sound tempting? And he ate it up. He was still on a post-shag high, yearning to spend more time with the woman who captivated him and whose arse fit spectacularly in his hands. He needed to get a grip. Like taking a moment to relieve his pesky mortal needs and find the sound of that running water to freshen up his manky state.

Sliding his hand back along the marble wall, he found water falling from a stone-carved head, by the feel of it. "Not bad," he muttered at the delightfully not freezing water and scrubbed his face around the blindfold and splashed water on his body. But he couldn't wash away one gnawing thought. This was no typical morning after a one-night stand or casual affair.

Medusa was a warm-blooded woman from an ancient world. He reached to his right, patting the air until he landed on cloth. Not unlike how he blindly felt his way through an unexpected relationship, with feelings that threw him off balance. He'd left things like dating, friends, family, hell, his whole career behind, searching for proof he was right and his brother and everyone in his life had been wrong.

Stillness sank into his chest along with doubt.

He'd come for proof even if it killed him, leaving all his evidence at the inn with instructions, if he didn't return after a week, to send it to an old friend, now a journalist. He shuddered, sickened by how close he'd come to making Medusa's life even worse. Just like he'd bollixed up his own life and his relationship with his brother.

"Breakfast is served."

Her voice never failed to drag him from the abyss of guilt, resentment, and all those other pesky dark feelings he failed to repress.

"Maybe I don't deserve this, you, all you've shared with me, and last night. I don't deserve your love."

"You regret the sex?"

Her flat tone neatly sliced through the wounds he'd already reopened.

"No, definitely not! I haven't had such a brilliant shag maybe ever. But this is more than sex, this thing between us. And it's not something I've done well. Or at all without mucking it up."

"Jason, you don't have to—"

"Yes, I bloody do," he insisted. Arms crossed and feeling a touch vulnerable, naked, he struggled through the talking-of-feelings bit, which was usually where he ruined relationships.

"You've been a victim for millennia, attacked, not exactly properly wooed. And I know you were worried about being rough with me earlier, but I'm the one who could have, you know, hurt you."

She burst out in laughter. "Dear Jason, you saw the evidence of what I do to trespassers. Do you realize how close you were to becoming my latest decoration?"

"Well, me dying was part of the initial plan, but so was leaving behind my notes at the inn as proof, thus making me posthumously published and revered." He scratched at his jaw, wincing at his self-revelation on how much of a prat he was. "Which now sounds pretentious and—" He let loose a drawn-out groan. "I'm no better than those idiots looking for internet fame!"

"Jason, you might have wanted to make your mark

with what many may consider a foolish plan, but you're not an idiot. You didn't fall to my curse. Instead, you did what no one else even thought of. Treated me with respect and a curiosity that kept you coming back to me." Her firm grip on his elbow gently guided him forward.

He snorted in response to her generous comment. "I'm not so noble as you make me out to be. You deserve someone worthy of love, someone who hasn't shoved everyone in his life away and settled into his own selfish obsession."

"Worthy is overrated. And I'm liking the obsession. It brought you here."

He fought back a smile even as he wanted to scoff at her flirting.

"Best decision of my life even if it was a touch on the self-serving side." He leaned into her as she nudged him to lower onto the slightly scratchy fabric-covered ground. He sat cross-legged, feeling quite comfortable even as naked as the day he was born. Not necessarily a nudist, him, but it was just him and her there, and he certainly hadn't hesitated to bare his ass the prior night. A cocky grin broke through his guilt and earlier self-loathing. Maybe, if he was lucky, he'd earn a round two, christening the picnic blanket again.

She brushed her lips against his temple. "Don't move."

A breeze cooled his shoulder where she'd warmed his skin. But more than lust gave him the lapping heat washing across his body. How she curled her tall frame against him the previous night, intimately tangling their bodies, had been a comfort.

Well, more than a comfort. Something he wanted more of. He'd visualized in his mind how they must look, spooned together, her silky olive-toned skin pressed against him, snakes and black braids draped across her shoulders. Her sketches had hinted at the beautiful woman who no one could gaze upon. But Medusa was far more than a sketch or legend. Each brush of soft lips, the way she smiled against his shoulder, and the musical hiss of her snakes belied beauty poets would write epic poems about.

The blindfold protected him from her curse but hadn't made him any less aroused. Touching and skimming his hands across her body, mapping out every curve, was erotic in a way he'd never imagined. He was half stiff, thinking about her.

He was a lusty bastard for sure. One brush of his hand on metal and denim reminded him if he mucked up the post-sex chat or the whole persuading to indulge a little morning delight, at least he didn't have to make a naked runner. Although running from Medusa brought a dull ache in his chest.

Splashing sounds and the clinking of meal prep elicited an odd pang of yearning. Maybe it was a reminder of his parents and a happier time in his life. Or it was yet another sign affirming how domesticity in the temple was a thing he might get used to.

She placed a warm cup in his hands.

He inhaled an earthy, herbal scent. "Tea," he acknowledged and enjoyed a sip of a sweeter almost anise version of what he was used to. "Thank you."

"I'm not asking for anything more than last night. I just want you to know I understand if you can't stay," she said quickly like she wanted to get it out. Not unlike his *thanks for the shag, got to run* speech he'd given too many times.

Being on the receiving end, though, that was new, and his gut clenched at the thought of leaving and not returning. Worse was that niggling doubt about his initial motivations for finding her. He'd come to Greece looking for vindication, but he'd found something more important.

"Medusa, love, I'm not going anywhere."

"You don't understand. I can never leave this place. Death would follow along with terror, and I would turn into something I don't want to be. And this place isn't safe for you." Her voice caught.

"What if it's where I want to be?" he interrupted and blindly reached for her until his hand landed on the smooth skin of her knee. "Yes, it's dangerous, but—and I really hate saying this—but me finding you, maybe it's fate or the gods at work." He grimaced at that thought. "I'm not one who believes in fate. My parents, how they died, led me on this journey to you."

Her hip bumped against his until they settled close together, skin to skin.

"Fate is a tricky concept, my love." She sighed and pressed a section of orange to his lips.

He bit down, enjoying the sweet, acidic juice.

"Tell me about your parents."

"A bit of a morbid topic after such a brilliant night."

"Jason." She drew his name out and swept fingers through his hair. "You know so much about me. And if your parents are part of our fate, I'd like to know. You did say you thought they were killed by Olympians."

She bribed him with leftover stuffed grape leaves.

His mum and dad had been gone for twenty-three years. Except for him, as long as he focused on his work, their work, they were still with him. A storm of emotions roiled and thundered into a pounding like the ocean that had stolen his parents' life. If one person would understand his obsession over who and what took their lives, it was Medusa.

"My parents were the most loving, warm, and brilliant people I've ever known. We lived in Oxford then. During the day, they ran a local apothecary and market. At night, they audited courses on Prehistoric Britain, Archaeological Finds and Prehistoric Tools, and a few on mythology and theology of ancient cultures. Sometimes my mum would read to me from whatever she was studying."

"No wonder you have such a love of the past," she gushed.

"Maybe," he acknowledged. "Or maybe it was because my brother loathed history, and I was keen on annoying him and being my parents' favorite." He could smile now. Years—hell, decades ago—he'd used his brother's intolerant attitude as a weapon. "I was already at uni and not exactly focused but leaning toward teaching and research when I lost them. You see, they were on an archaeological dig on a beach on the Welsh Coast, investigating evidence of Atlantis."

"Not the safest topic in the Olympian Realm," she noted.

Tension twisted like a vice in his shoulders. Resentment surfaced as sharp and bitter as the day they'd died and he'd screamed his rage at the sea. "You mean they were killed over the lost city by petty Olympians?" He snorted and sank into the bitterness that always hovered. Even when he taught Olympian mythology to his students, his anger had seeped out in mockery of twisted, debauched tales. Another reason he'd lost his job and delved a little too passionately into his favorite dark topics.

"You said they died on the shore?" she prompted.

"After one particularly bad storm, a few stone artifacts were uncovered. They rushed to the site with a few enthusiasts who shared their curiosity. They'd invited me down, but I had exams." He paused, swallowing hard at the welling emotions. The guilt that he hadn't been there to protect them still ached. "They should have been fine. The sea was calm, and it was a sunny beautiful day at low tide. The authorities said it was a freak wave that swept ashore, drowning them and their team."

She went silent. The only sound slicing through the thick sadness that descended was seagulls screeching from outside the temple. Finally, after he wondered if he'd reminded her of things she wanted to forget, she spoke.

"I'm so sorry, Jason." She squeezed his arm and brushed her lips on his temple.

"So it was them," he stated with a sharp edge he didn't mean to direct at her.

"There was an Atlantean war against Poseidon long before I met him. Few talk about it. All I can tell you is that one day Atlantis existed in this realm, and the next, a new mortal realm formed, Atlantea, and every trace of Atlantis vanished from this realm."

He sat in stunned silence before slowly responding. "My mum and dad died because they almost proved a rebel city existed. The irony of my life paralleling theirs is a bit on the nose." He reached to rake a hand through his hair still bound by the blindfold. It reminded him of the constraints on his life he always fought against and frustrated him.

"I'm sorry. The gods are often fickle and vengeful to protect their precious honor." She spit the words out as sharp and angry as he felt.

"My parents died together for what they believed in," he admitted, staring into the black fabric, imagining them holding each other as they faced the sea. "Losing them set the course for my life. My brother." He snorted. "He said I should move on like he did. Cold fish, that one. All business. He buried them and acted like they never existed. Accused me of wasting my life like they had. He always resented their career. And me for following them. I said things to him that were not exactly an example of brotherly love. Holidays were hell. Easier for me to be on my own."

"Do you regret leaving him behind?"

His head snapped toward her, and he sat upright. His Medusa had a keen understanding of human nature and his feelings. "No and yes. Sometimes I feel I pissed away my duty to uphold whatever family my parents made for us. Especially my mum. I know she'd be raging at the two of us. But then I remember what a bloody twat he is. He'd never understand this, you and me. My parents would."

"They'd...bless us?" she asked tentatively.

"I think they would," he admitted, and again his thoughts drifted to the chain of events that had led him to her.

A thud and clank sounded on the balcony, interrupting the more serious direction things had taken away from a night of sex and playful fun.

"That would be Hermes making his deliveries. He's got the worst aim." She lifted away from him in a hiss of her snakes. "If I don't fetch the tribute baskets now, the rats and seagulls will mass. It's like an apocalypse. I'll get a lecture scroll about duty and how it's not all defend the temple. Then the Olympian bureaucrats will send me inventories, and it's just unpleasant. Be right back."

"Olympian bureaucrats. Some things never change."

He felt around for more breakfast, now far hungrier after unloading emotional baggage about his parents. Funny how the pain dulled after talking to her. On a more basic level, he did need energy if he was going to keep up with his amorous gorgon. A huge grin stretched across his face as he found leftover pastry. Maybe his parents were smiling down on him now.

Bells chimed in an eerie reminder of when he'd first entered the temple. Medusa had a visitor, the kind that came to challenge her rather than indulge in pleasant conversation.

A chill swept through him that had nothing to do with the damp, aged atmosphere in the temple. He had only two choices, and one would endanger his lover. Either from injury or the trauma of ending another life.

No. The word resonated through him. Medusa had teased he was not the typical hero. But he was stubborn, and if nothing else, he had the tall, broad-shouldered build to capture attention. He'd talked his way out of a few uncomfortable legal issues about archaeological sites and private property. Not to mention he'd thwarted a few scavengers and grave robbers. That gave him the advantage. He'd have the temple trespasser sorted before Medusa had to unleash her curse. Easy peasy.

Chapter Nine

With an abundance of confidence and an unrelenting need to protect Medusa, he quickly pulled on his jeans and reached for the blindfold. Should he, though?

She'd asked him to keep it on. Somehow facing a possibly armed trespasser while blindfolded didn't appeal. It ruined the whole *protective boyfriend about to lecture the intruder disturbing archaeological sites* vibe he was counting on.

He unknotted the band and then stuffed it into his pocket and blinked through the dim light. He raked a hand through his hair before feeling a smile tug at his lips. The well-shagged, disheveled look wasn't exactly intimidating, but he'd work with it.

Squaring his shoulders, he marched his way toward the entrance, weaving around the stone statues of the dead. "Hallo!" he called out before letting loose a series of sneezes. "She wasn't kidding about the dust," he muttered.

"Don't even breathe, mate, or I'll drop you where you stand."

A familiar London accent in a sharp pissed-off feminine voice rang out. The petite blonde dressed in a pink T-shirt and denim shorts looked out of place. So did the assault rifle with a mobile attached on the sight on top of the barrel, which she pointed at him.

He slowly raised his hands. "Steady now, I'm not

armed." He gestured down at his bare chest, jeans, and bare feet. "Dr. Jason Walker, here studying archaeological evidence in this temple." He kept his distance. "You caught me during breakfast, which in this place isn't always the safest."

"Where's Drake?" The woman's voice held a hint of accusation. She pointed the black metal weapon at him with an unnerving calm.

"Sorry, there's no Drake here," he said slowly, contemplating his options and how much time he had before Medusa returned.

"He came here investigating this cult. What did you do to him?"

Fuck. This was not good.

"I think you might have the wrong temple. There's no one here unless you count these brilliant statues."

"Shut it. I know he's here. He posted two days ago outside this temple and hasn't uploaded since. Tell me where he is. Now."

She didn't flinch in her demand. How her finger curled around the trigger caused his heart to pound. He might have laid on a sarcastic quip if she didn't already broadcast such a mad vibe. Any other place or circumstance, he'd find it difficult to take her seriously. Especially when she scowled and loosened her grip on the gun to tap the screen of her sparkly encrusted mobile phone, and muttered about *rubbish bars*.

A snide comment burned on his tongue to lecture this girl who, like many of his ex-students, suffered from an inability to function without a lifeline to the internet. Taunting someone who might accidentally shoot him didn't seem wise.

"Miss—"

"Angel4670 and I'm recording all of this even if I can't get a signal."

Heartburn the likes of which he hadn't experienced since his teaching days scalded the center of his chest. He swallowed down his disdain for social media and donned his teaching voice. "Angel, you don't mind if I call you that?"

"Yeah, whatever." She kept the gun aimed at him as she tapped her phone once more.

He lowered his hands to his sides and let loose a calming breath. "This place isn't safe. Much of the structure is unstable. I've been here for the past two days, and there's no one else here. Just me and my research on this very cursed temple, which I'd encourage you to take seriously. These statues around us weren't carved. They were people once. You and I are both at risk of joining them."

"Do you think I'm stupid?" She lunged forward until the black metal barrel gouged into his chest.

He flinched, and the first inklings of doubt tightened his neck. So much for his grand plan at de-escalation. Time to change tactics. Or risk losing everything he was, even now, admitting he'd gained. He was not one to pray, but he did nonetheless that Medusa stayed out of the line of fire.

"Angel, I can't help you if I'm bleeding out from a bullet wound." He spoke forcefully and calmly. "If you're sure he's here—"

"He's here. I told you he uploaded from out front, and we all saw it. Now stop lying and tell your cult friends to let him go. We know all about you sickos. It's why my boyfriend came here. He posted all about it. So don't give me that curse shite. Hear that? You cult

101

nutters! It's not working!" she shouted.

He flinched at the cold metal digging in the center of his chest. When she commenced screeching for Drake, the sound drilled into his head.

Never in all the things he thought might go wrong with Medusa had a dangerous, off-her-nut, grieving girlfriend been on the list. He clenched his jaw and tried not to aggravate the woman with a ponytail swinging and several emoji tattoos on her arm.

He was prepared to die for a lot of things. This was not one of them. Unless it was protecting Medusa, which appealed to his original intent at a noble demise. Then again, as Angel screamed about follower count and likes, his head began to pound. *Bloody hell.* This had to be some kind of punishment.

"Angel, here's a thought. Maybe your bloke found something more interesting to blog about? This curse is ancient history." He tried hard not to smirk at his own joke.

"Blogging is so last decade. This is TikTok, arsehole, and don't start up about that curse bollocks. Drake's a top star on any platform, and he was about to expose all of you and your moonlight orgies. What did you do? Make him your sex slave?"

"What? No! No sex slaves here." Unless he counted his randy thoughts for Medusa. His face ached with the effort it took not to laugh at the ludicrous accusations. He had a feeling Medusa would get the humor if it weren't for the gun pointed at him.

Angel's angular face pinched, and her light-blue eyes turned hard. Until she glanced over his shoulder. "Drake!"

He turned as she raced to a statue just behind him.

"No, it can't be!"

He felt a fragment of relief when she slung the gun on her shoulder and wept loudly on a fresh stone statue of a young man dressed in cargo shorts and T-shirt.

"You even killed his mobile." She dropped to the ground and cradled the dust-covered phone before launching upward and again whipping around. He found himself in the line fire as she advanced forward, gun barrel inches from his chest.

He raised his palms toward her and again wondered what he'd done to deserve this. No, he knew what he'd done. Ignored his brother. Quit his students after telling the administration to kiss his arse, and then ran headlong into the dangerous myth of Medusa without a thought about anyone except him.

"Shooting me isn't going to bring him back." His heart raced, and with every beat, he knew he had to get the gun away from her.

"Murderer!" she shouted. Her voice cracked, and her hands shook. "You and your sickos did this!"

"How the bloody hell would I turn someone to stone?" He tried reason. The truth felt more dangerous. Facing the unstable woman narrating and crying into the phone attached to the rifle epitomized every reason he'd stopped teaching.

His temper frayed, and anger heated his neck. He wasn't going to die and especially not this way. He'd die his way and protect Medusa.

Adrenaline swelled as he lunged for the barrel. She yanked and twisted, struggling with him. Jason's feet skidded on the dust-covered floor.

"Put the gun down," he said as sweat beaded, and his fingers tightened on the cold metal barrel. He shoved her backward against poor, cursed, stone Drake.

A loud bang was followed by pain lancing his left shoulder. Everything slowed and muffled. Her mouth moved, but he was too busy hitting the ground to hear her. Pain crushed at his chest until he could barely breathe.

"No!" Medusa's voice boomed in the temple, piercing the pounding in his ears.

Something wet and sticky cooled on his chest.

"Come out, you fucking monster!" Angel shrieked off to his side. "Or I'll do worse than bleed him."

He fought back nausea cramping his stomach and chills racking his body. After inhaling a painful breath, he dug deep for willpower to stop the mad blogger from hurting Medusa. "Angel, don't do this. It's not going to bring him back."

"Shut up! You and your monster are dead! Me and my followers will see to it!"

His vision was turning gray, and words eluded him as he fought through the darkness clutching at the edges of his vision.

"If she wants a monster, let her have one." Medusa's voice deepened and hissed until the sound burned across his skin, and the ground shook beneath him. He heard Angel scream one last time before the world faded to darkness, and he plunged into a sweet abyss.

Chapter Ten

Millennia of instincts rushed through Medusa at the crack of a gunshot. The soft curves and smiling face of a lover turned into hardened rage. Her curse consumed reason, propelling her to pass judgment on those who violated the sanctity of her temple. Except this time, it was far more personal. The intruder hurt her Jason.

Power roared through Medusa like a howling storm at sea. She embraced the maelstrom until dust and shards of marble rained around her. Each step, her heart simmered with rage until her snakes thrashed and hissed.

The stone forest of her victims shattered as the young blonde woman aimed her weapon of choice at Medusa.

Jason's collapsed form sowed the fate of this pathetic mortal trespasser. The girl wanted a monster. So Medusa fulfilled her wish with a sadistic pleasure that shivered up her spine.

"No one hurts my Jason." Never had she relished ending a life as she did this one. Her pulse raced in giddy delight as the girl screamed.

Medusa didn't burn with regret or cry or turn away this time.

Until her gaze landed on Jason lying so still, blood pooling on his chest and dripping onto the stone floor.

"No." Her throat thickened and coated with dust, almost choking her. The world seemed to tilt until her knees buckled.

"Jason." Tears blurred her vision, but one fact stopped her from collapsing onto his chest.

He wore no blindfold.

Panic stole her breath as she scurried backward, bare feet kicking at dust and crumbled marble. She turned, and her gaze landed on the remnants of their picnic.

Basket and cups went flying as she yanked the blanket up and wrapped it around her head.

This was her punishment. The brutal reality of her curse carved into her flesh like shards of marble. Nothing she could do would save him. He was dying on her temple floor.

Helplessness and fear sliced deep through her chest. This wasn't like any other who died there. It wasn't her curse, but it was still her responsibility. Jason stayed for her, loved her, and wanted to protect her.

Deep in her soul, the ache spread until sorrow weighted her limbs and clenched at her heart at what she must do.

Their time, her love and hopes, were a fantasy that had almost killed him. Now, she would do what she should have done from the beginning.

Outside, in the mortal world, he would survive. Swallowing back her grief and guilt, she grabbed his shirt tossed carelessly the prior night. She sank to her knees by his side and tied the shirt around his shoulder.

It blossomed scarlet with his blood.

"Medusa." He groaned, and his pale face contorted in pain.

She soothed him, drawing her fingers across his sweat-slicked forehead. "Promise me you'll live." She grasped at every ounce of strength to keep her voice steady. Her snakes hissed in misery. They too felt the loss of this man who had quickly become important in her life.

"Only if you will," he murmured, his eyelids flickering to a slitted opening before falling shut.

She secured the blanket over her head tighter and lifted him, slinging his good arm around her shoulder. Satisfied he was safe from her curse, she half dragged him from the temple, stumbling and tripping down the gravel path. Despite a gorgon's strength, she struggled, not with his bulky frame, but with the weight of her emotions. Every step led to pain and loss. Only his heartbeat mattered. If that stopped, she was afraid of what she might do.

One more step to keep him safe, she promised herself, dragging him down toward the dock.

Charon's raspy cursing finally ended the arduous trek. "Have you lost your gorgon mind!"

"You will take him to safety."

"Hades would have him if you'd just finish him off. He could be off doing... Well, depends on how he died now, doesn't it?"

"No." Still covered, she peeked past the blanket's edge to watch the black-robed ferryman turn and cower in the old wooden skiff. "I already gave Hades a soul this day. You will take Jason to the island and call on Eros." She paused and fought the acidic burning pain in her chest. "And you will not bring Jason Walker back to these shores. He's paid enough tribute to this temple."

"This is highly irregular! Against the rules! And Eros?" He let loose a raspy groan. "He doesn't associate with my type. Not his gig if you know what I mean. And do you know the pain inflicted on me for disobeying my master by saving a life? It's not part of my job description, and he might—"

"I've given you plenty of souls to more than satisfy your duty. Now take him and go before I unleash my curse on you. I doubt Hades would be pleased to see his ferryman so in need of saving." Medusa found it easier to threaten, to cling to the bitterness and anger she channeled to destroy trespassers. It shielded her aching heart.

She gave her lover one last look, kneeling by his side. She brushed her lips across his cooling forehead. "I will love you forever. Please live for both of us."

The wind gusted, lifting at the blanket as she turned back to her temple, unable to watch Jason leave her.

Dark clouds swirled, and an ominous thunder rolled. Her nails bit into her palms as she fought power welling in her to be released. Instead, she listened to the ferryman grumble and drag Jason onto the skiff. Followed by the splash and creak of old wood on the ocean.

Tears wet her cheeks before the first stinging pelt of rain hit her shrouded head.

Only when the rhythmic splash of the ferryman faded did she let the blanket fall to the gravel.

Grief turned to rage at her loss.

She held her arms wide as her snakes whipped and sizzled with the power she unleashed. Screaming into the storm, she allowed her pain freedom until seagulls dropped from the sky, shattering onto the ground. Her voice turned hoarse until she dropped to her knees, rocks biting into her skin. Pain. It was the one constant in her life. Along with a dark, empty temple. Her heart shattered, and shivering in the rain, she retreated back to her duty with nothing but sorrow as her companion.

Chapter Eleven

Hot needle-like pain jabbed Jason in the shoulder until he opened his eyes. He squinted through a pounding headache until a familiar blond-haired god leaned over him.

"Took you long enough. You've been out of it for hours."

Eros' familiar voice pierced the numbing gray fog of unconsciousness. He swallowed hard against nausea and brain fog. When he tried to sit up, half his body screamed in pain until Jason accepted this wasn't just a hangover.

He was in a bland white-walled room with an IV hooked up to his right arm. His breath hitched at memories of a blonde girl and a gun.

"Medusa, I've got to go back—" His body wouldn't cooperate as he tried to haul himself out of bed. Nearly blacking out, he fell back, almost knocking the IV pouch on its metal hanger to the floor.

"You're in no shape to go anywhere," Eros said with an annoyingly amused tone. "And she sent you away so you wouldn't die on her floor. Good thing I like you. I had to call in favors to get you here. Charon wasn't happy, and I've already gotten a stern warning from Lord Hades. Not that I'm worried. I was on his side with the whole thing with Persephone."

Jason took in the sling and bulky white gauze

bandages wrapped around his left shoulder. "There was a girl. She shot me. Where am I? I need to make sure Medusa—" Pain ripped across his chest. His stomach threatened to heave its contents.

"You're at the local hospital. Not more than a clinic really, but they stitched you up well enough. And I'll be taking that thank you now."

The cocky Olympian stood like the golden-haired legend he was, arms crossed, gazing down at Jason. If he wasn't already suffering, Jason would have had some clever retort. Unfortunately, pain medications and a bullet wound made just staying conscious a struggle.

"Thank you, but technically, Medusa saved me first. I need to get back and make sure she's safe. We were attacked by a lovesick social-media type." He groaned at the memory, and then the penny dropped. She'd had a cell phone on the gun. "She recorded me. I've got to stop the video from posting."

Eros let loose deep rolling laughter. Jason shifted on the bed, annoyance heating his aching chest as he sucked in a deep breath. He strained aching muscles to lever himself upright and gave the god his best scowling glare. Which made Eros laugh harder.

"It's not funny. One video and Medusa won't have a chance. She'll be mobbed by hordes of people, and not just the influencer types. She could be hurt." Jason had a shuddering well of fear of what worse could be in the modern world. Turning her into a commodity or weapon. He'd die before allowing that to happen. "I need to make sure no one else finds her."

"Jason, my lad, finding her is part of the gig. They walk in, and she curses them. She's handled that task for thousands of your years."

"That's why I should be there and why I need to go back. That mobile is a ticking bomb waiting to go off. She shouldn't have to deal with that alone, not when I can shut the damned thing off, erase it, or bloody destroy it." He slumped back as oxygen seemed in short supply, and his skin turned clammy.

"Your lack of faith in her and my ability to manage nosy mortals and their technology is insulting." The fluorescent lights flickered as Eros hurled words like his infamous arrows.

Maybe pain or the drugs dripping into his veins gave him a delusional confidence until Jason lost all sense of self-preservation. "It's not about you or insults. She's on that island alone. She doesn't need to be ending hordes of pillocks who'll show up." He growled in frustration and reached a hand toward the burning pain underneath his bandage.

Eros knocked it away. "I'm giving you a break because you're a wounded, lovesick idiot. To clarify for your drug-addled brain, I'm not putting up with anyone interfering with my project. That would be you and her. Especially not mortals publicizing Olympian existence for their own glory.

"No one on Olympus will be used to plump up ungrateful greedy mortals. Not without a decent amount of tribute first. Something your people haven't done in ages. A little thanks and a new temple would be nice. I haven't had a decent festival dedicated to me in ages."

Jason ignored the vain god's petulant complaints. His thoughts centered on Medusa, how she'd suffer for ending another life. Once again, he'd failed the whole hero gig. Maybe he deserved to be shot. The pain had to be less than she was feeling after his blunder.

"I should be there to hold her and be reassuring." Not stuck in a hospital listening to Eros whinge. Lying here was a direct result of his stunning inability to defeat an opponent with his so-called intelligence. Now he understood how much of a clueless git he'd been. He'd been so undeservedly cocky when he first entered her temple.

That had been three days ago. The best days of his life. Until he'd ended up in a hospital.

"Oh, stop it. The whole self-pitying funk isn't helping, and it's annoying. Yes, you should be with her. But not throwing yourself in front of bullets. Although points for nobility. So are you ready to admit your feelings and that I was spot on with the blindfold?"

Jason wanted to tell him to piss off. Kind of hard to do when one raspy inhale ended in a coughing fit and another spasm of clawing pain. He hated to admit it, but a thread of truth lingered in what Eros took credit for. Jason did love her. And for the first time in his normally solitary life, he didn't want to be alone.

"She means more than you can understand." Like how he'd rather be recovering in a damp, crumbling temple than a proper bed. The compulsion drew at him, like an invisible force drawing him to do something other than lie there. Pushing past pain and shaking muscles, he swung his legs over the side of the bed.

The bed sank when Eros sat next to him, stretching denim clad legs before him. "Jason, you romantic sod. That's why I like you. One in a million, you are. If anyone understands intense passion, the love worth taking a bullet for, it's me."

The teasing in Eros' voice grated on Jason's already raw emotions.

"She's worth more and deserves better than me. All I wanted was to spare her from another death, from the guilt. That's what you do for the people you love." The power of his declaration seemed to press inward until the air practically thickened. Admitting his love out loud in the mortal world could be dangerous. It felt odd coming from him. But good, saying it and meaning it. Not in some flowery or disingenuous way. But genuinely feeling the connection and rightness.

He eyed the god next to him. Maybe Eros was the only one who understood how foreign the declaration was to Jason.

"A sacrifice," Eros drew out softly, now less the playful antagonist. He gave Jason enough of a penetrating look to make him squirm worse than the pain tearing across his chest.

"No, that's not what this is." Jason hated admitting he'd followed instincts rather than thought about the ancient world interpretation. Suddenly, his thoughts turned to how Medusa would think about his rash actions. "She wouldn't want me to die," he admitted softly.

"As you wanted to save her. She felt the same. One lover sacrificing for the other." Eros tilted his head. "This is better than a keg of Persephone's best ambrosia. I haven't been this tingly and exhilarated since a particularly raunchy Lupercalia in Terra over a thousand years ago."

"I need to get back. To make it clear that I—" What would he say? He'd already revealed so much, given her bits of himself, his past he'd not shared with anyone. In three days, he'd fallen harder for her than anyone he'd dated for three weeks, which was pretty much his limit.

Not with Medusa, though.

"I need to make sure she understands it wasn't just sex or curiosity or my obsession with her mythology."

"If I've got this right, you two definitely shagged, and you took a bullet playing the hero for her. She knows why. Just like she knows you're mortal and belong in this mortal realm. She's not meant to be part of your world. That's who we are, Jason. We live beyond you, know more, see more, and live far longer than your brief blip of life. You gave her a love she'll cherish."

The arrogant challenge of Eros' words fueled a stubborn streak Jason was known for. It had kept him going after his parents died. He'd channeled it to publish his work and teach. It had driven him to leave London behind, tell his brother to piss off, and to find answers and uncover the truth of the ancient myths.

"It's not enough." He levered himself off the bed. The room tilted as he shifted his bound arm so he could begin picking at medical tape around the IV shunt. "You, the gods, or whatever else is at work here set me on this path. I may have bumbled into her temple, giving you and yours a laugh, but she and I connected and changed each other for the better. I can't walk away from that."

"Don't go blaming me for your obsessions. As amusing as they are. You found her, somehow lived, earned her affection, and then asked for my blessing. Being my generous self, I gave both of you a glimpse of what you could have. Impossible love happened, and I helped nudge you along. Quite an achievement given…well, you're you." He rose up and leveled another godly stare at Jason who didn't flinch.

Standing his ground, he continued his battle against the adhesive, ready to rip it off and storm past whatever the fickle gods tossed in his way. Eros clamped onto his wrist, stilling Jason's jerky movements.

"Now see here, *mortal*. I've done my part. But fate's a different deal. Even gods can't control that. Mortal choice is powerful. Annoying as it is, you made a choice inserting yourself between her and the latest to storm the temple. You rolled the dice and lost."

Jason yanked his arm away, hissing at racking pain shooting across his body. "Don't lecture me about choice. My parents didn't choose to die. I didn't choose to be miserable or get shot."

"Seriously?" he barked out.

"I'm not naive. I see the connection. What your kind did to my parents twisted me up inside until I had to prove the Olympians existed. My choice was to find the truth no matter the cost, and Medusa was part of that. But meeting her changed me. I may not be sappy or spouting poetry, but even if I only have another forty years, I'd rather spend them blindfolded with her in a dusty temple, fending off idiots who invade her space. She's worth everything. You can either help me or get out of the way."

He yanked tape off, grunting as hair and possibly a layer of skin came off with it. Eros grabbed his good shoulder as his knees wobbled.

"From eternal bachelor enjoying dalliances right into permanent love." Eros' smile stretched across his annoying perfectly sculpted jaw until his eyes twinkled.

Jason felt the first flutter of nerves.

"You continue to pay off my investment in this relationship. Forever is beyond the favor granted to you. But doable if you're willing. You see, my dear foolish mortal, if I help you find a path leading to a lifetime with her, you will pay a heavy price."

"I'll pay it." Foolish to say to a mercurial Olympian who could torment him. Jason no longer wanted to play around. His mind was made up. And his arse needed to get in gear before he passed out.

"Lovesick fools are a favorite of mine. But I need more than your impulses and hormones driving the deal. I want a genuine conscious choice. A true sacrifice based on thought and emotion and not impulse. You have one night. Think hard, Jason. There's no going back, no do-overs once you go down this path."

Eros, the infamous Erik Valentine, squeezed his shoulder before stepping away, practically rubbing his hands together with an eye-crinkling smile spreading across his face. One that Jason was sure had melted many a heart and maybe flushed through him in ways he didn't want to admit. But beyond that surge of godly induced pheromones, he teetered on the edge of uncertainty. Not about Medusa, but Eros hurling words like fate, choice, and sacrifice.

"I'll call the nurse. You heal, have a nice meal, and think."

"I won't change my mind."

"A true clearheaded choice is worth more to me. Free will, faith, and cutting a deal with me, especially for impossible love, plumps my reputation. Not to mention the bragging rights. And Athena's not the most understanding if I interfere. I'll be taking a hit for you and Medusa. Athena doesn't forget transgressions. Trust me, I learned that the hard way."

A dark-haired nurse in purple scrubs entered the room and sighed. "You shouldn't be up."

"Good luck, Dimitra. This one is a handful. Make

sure he eats and gets a good night's rest."

Jason allowed the stronger-than-she-looked nurse to ease him back to bed. He flinched after she fussed with his IV. But he had more on his mind than a needle in his arm or drugs that kept him stuck in a hospital. Eros' casual comment about godly retribution raised memories of his parents' deaths and, worse, Medusa's fate. Interfering Olympians like Athena could stop him, rip them apart, or worse. Maybe that's why he'd been shot.

Having Eros on his side might be the best bet. Then again, could one trust any of these fickle gods? With that thought and a nurse softly chastising him in Greek, he lay back on the bed as whatever sedatives she had added to his IV sent him into sleep and dreams of a dark temple and the soft hiss of snakes in his ear as he slept next to his Medusa.

Chapter Twelve

Overlooking the rubble cluttering her temple, Medusa drew her fingertips across her dust-covered cheek. Shadows stretched ominously over the evidence of her rage. She rolled the grit between her thumb and finger, which she then wiped off on her skirts.

Past the fiery rage and heartbreak, a dull ache still lingered from the loss that carved a void in her soul. Aimlessly, she wandered, dragging bare feet through thick crumbles of stone until she reached the balcony and the sea. Slick with sea spray, she stared out at the swelling water, dark and angry as she had been.

The unfairness of it all shattered the hardened wall she'd erected in an attempt to stave off gut-wrenching sadness. She'd served Athena and fulfilled her duty for over two thousand years. She'd prayed and begged for forgiveness. When she met Jason, she'd thought perhaps she'd find absolution through a mortal who loved without judgment.

Now all she felt was another painful lesson which had been dispensed. An emptiness sat cold and heavy, leaching the essence that made her Medusa.

Tears would not come. She'd cried so many already.

"Looks like Troy after the siege."

The annoying voice of Eros cut through her misery, reigniting rage. He made a decent target to vent at. She whipped around, snakes hissing and vibrating with power.

"Easy now. Or I might change my mind."

"About what?" She hissed the words, not unlike her snakes. Rushing forward, she hunted the teasing god who would never know even a fraction of her misery.

"The broken mortal you sent me, who still yearns for you."

His elusive voice taunted her, seemingly echoing among columns and rafters until the flutter of wings beat through the temple. As she often did with more lethal intruders, she silently slipped past stone and marble, taking in the air heavy with dust and sea mist.

"His injury is your fault as much as mine. The blindfold tempted both of us, offering a night of pleasure. A lie that ended in false happiness and my obligation to do what I always do. Except this time, he was just as much the victim. That's what you do. You toy with people's lives for your own amusement." Her voice lost the velvety quality she'd enjoyed with her lover. Now she channeled the mythic quality of her gorgon family, rumbling and deep meant to terrorize a victim. After all, that's what she was, the monster who ended fools who entered her temple.

"Fun is not watching one of my favorite mortals bleed out. And exhibit all the loathsome stubborn qualities that kept him from my influence for so many years," he grumbled, and thuds and scrapes of rubble were followed by cursing in a display of godly temper. "Pain in my arse, he is. And then there's you throwing a goddess-level tantrum. If I wanted this level of aggravation, blood, and petulant attitudes, I'd be at Olympus, drinking away my misery while listening to Mother complain about mortals disrespecting her."

119

"Then why come here? Or do you get perverse kicks out of us risking our hearts, his life, and the petty vengeance that followed for daring to—" She couldn't finish that sentence. A wave of soul-crushing misery consumed her until she sank to her knees. She pressed the heel of her hand to her mouth to control heaving sobs that had consumed her after she'd destroyed every last reminder of her curse that still stood in the temple.

"I'm here, dear Medusa, because I'm not so jaded or self-involved as my mother. Or a vapid god basking in pettiness. I want to feel passion, thrive in it, and maybe if I'm lucky, get some credit. That's why this impossible love of you two drew me in like a moth to a flame. It's dangerous and thrilling. I might get burned as much as you and Jason."

"I doubt you risk that much," she spat out, refusing to give him any pleasure in her grief.

"You'd be surprised. Jason's right, you know. There's more than a little Olympian Realm influencing this realm. Someone's challenging me as much as you and your Jason."

Medusa dropped her hands and stood, pain replaced by outrage and a touch of revenge pouring through her like hot steel. "Who?"

"Could be my mum, Athena, the Fates, or any number of bored and vindictive deities."

His voice drifted on the wind, causing whirlwinds of dust at her feet.

"And how does the great Eros react to someone ruining his fun, stealing your triumph?"

"By winning, of course."

Blind fury drove her to stalk her temple, sliding around columns and sniffing the air for the myrrh-infused essence of an Olympian. Jason would never be safe if she didn't stop this.

"Jason's life isn't a game. And I won't play in some Olympian match, moving mortals around like toys. They may be annoying and foolish, but in this realm, they've made their own way. And Jason's life has been manipulated enough. He lost his parents to an Olympian vendetta over Atlantis. Isn't that enough?" She slowed and narrowed her eyes on a shadow stretched across the moonlit floor.

"Is that what he told you? Well now, that ups the ante, doesn't it?"

He disappeared as Medusa lunged forward to catch him.

"Nice try. Thanks for the info. And I promise you I'll be sussing out whoever may have toyed with our stubborn lout of a mortal. It's time to finish this game of mortal love and destiny. With a little help from me, of course. It'll be a sweet victory for everyone. That is—" He drew out the words, waiting on her, now from the other side of the temple.

Medusa clenched every muscle, hating this godly one-upmanship. Her face flashed hot, and a groan shook deep in her chest, but she had to know what he'd do. If nothing else, for Jason. "If what, love god?"

"Careful, sweetheart. I'm the one who's going to deliver up the potential for a happily ever after that'll shake the pillars of Olympus. Not to mention honk off some annoying holier-than-thou spoilsports."

"Eros, please don't do that." There it was, the tired drawl of a woman who had, not for the first time, listened to a god gleefully plot a triumph that could spectacularly backfire. This time, at her and Jason's expense.

"He loves you enough to do something reckless and stupid. I respect that. Maybe he inspires me."

Despite how her heart beat a little harder and she went soft and gooey inside, she also couldn't allow Jason to put himself in danger. "And I love him enough to do whatever I need to keep him safe. Even if it's to keep him away and never…" Her voice broke, and her chest grew tight. "See him again."

"You're actually touching me. I might actually have a twinge in my chest," he admitted with a playful pitch in his voice.

No longer worried about stealth, Medusa rushed forward, more determined to stop him no matter what.

"No, you've got to help Jason let it go. Even if you have to shoot him, give him someone else." And didn't that just burn a hole through her temples to the point even her snakes turned on her with a nip to her ear. She swatted them away.

"Won't work even if I wanted to. It's a pure, honest love he has for you. The kind I rarely get a taste of. If anything is worthy of my favor, it's this love. All I need from you, dear Medusa, is a promise to give it a chance. To give a little faith and maybe clean up this place." He sneezed and let loose a curse that Athena would frown at.

"Eros, please. Don't cause his life to end or shorten. Knowing he lives and enjoys all the mortal realm has to offer is what's keeping me going. I can endure another thousand years for knowing his love and that he lives on for both of us."

"You're going to be giving thanks to me. I'd like a spot of tribute out on the west balcony, before the setting sun. Snog him senseless and burn an oil lamp for me, a reminder of the truest most unusual love I've ever witnessed."

"Eros. This can't work."

"Dearest Gorgon, this is me. Now go freshen up and be sure to kiss him for me when next you see him."

"Eros don't you dare!" Medusa's shout rang through an empty temple.

She slumped down at the feet of Athena's statue towering over her. Only the soft hiss of her snakes comforted the dizzying spin of her thoughts.

At the heart of the maelstrom of love and fear was her Jason. The memory of his laughter, the delightful prickle of dark-gray stubble setting off his blue eyes, would always bring a sigh to her lips. How he'd tried to be heroic and face her enemies and fallen with a scowl on his face still thickened her throat and flushed her with a soft love. He'd called to her even injured, proving his thoughts centered on her as much as hers did on him.

Eros had that part right, how Jason bore a noble love, caring for her despite how bad she was for him. In all her long days cursing mortals, she'd never thought to find one who would capture her heart. Protecting him was what kept her going.

Eros dangled hope in front of her like one of Jason's delicious chocolates. Tears trailed down her dusty cheeks at the danger and that oh-so-seductive and tempting hope.

"Please, most honored Athena, do not punish Jason for any insult you take from careless words spoken by Eros or me. I will serve you without complaint for another thousand years if you will allow Jason to live."

Silently, she said another prayer to Eros to put Jason's well-being first and to allow their love to thrive throughout time. Or, if nothing else, as an inspiration for others. That even the most impossible relationships can happen in the darkest places.

She leaned back, her toe hitting something wet and sticky and awful. Her snakes hissed in mockery, thumping against her temple. A sigh escaped.

"Where's a god's favor when you need housekeeping?" she grumbled and scrubbed mashed pear off her toe with the hem of her gown.

Chapter Thirteen

Jason bolted upright, heart slamming in his chest. The remnants of his nightmare, the image of his parents swept out to sea, still left him shaken.

He reached to scrub at his face only to wince at searing pain radiating from his bound shoulder and arm. A few choice curses slipped out as he breathed through the pain. And the reality of how a nutter girl had shot him. Worse, Medusa had been forced to lay waste to another trespasser.

Guilt crushed down as he stared at medicinal white walls. One perfect night had turned into blood and death. So much for his less-than-stunning ability to use his intellect and gob to de-escalate armed intruders. No wonder his students hated him. Apparently, he was all talk and little substance.

"Valentine said you'd live. I had my doubts."

Setting aside self-pity, he licked dry lips and turned toward a teenaged girl sitting in a white plastic chair. She didn't look up, knitting needles clicking, entwined in hot-pink yarn.

"Where is he?" His throat felt as rough as sand paper, and if he had to wager, he looked as bad as he sounded. He wrenched himself to the side. Slowly, with measured movements he sat on the edge of the bed, breath coming in quick pants. He stifled a groan at stiff and aching muscles that stretched from head to toe.

"Typical man. First instinct is to demand, which I don't put up with, *English.* You're lucky I'm here." She spoke with a typical lyrical Greek accent but gave her words a hard edge.

His last nerve snapped. Frustration boiled up until sharp sarcasm ripped forth. "Look, miss." He struggled for polite.

Which the young dark-haired woman answered with a snort and raised brows.

"I've had a bugger of a day or days. I don't quite know at the moment because, oh yes, I've be shot."

"Yeah, you're an idiot." She stood up and shoved her knitting in a large woven handbag. "Before you start with the alpha-male crap, I already know where you were and what you were doing. You tried to be noble, and it turned to shit. Which was the obvious result to most people." She slid the bag onto her shoulder and crossed her arms, the picture of a defiant teenager in ripped jeans and a pink tank top.

Eros swept into the room. "Myrine, my dear favorite oracle!"

Jason wasn't sure if he should be relieved or annoyed. The girl seemed unfazed as the blond god filled the room with his charismatic presence. Jason's brain suddenly caught on to how Eros addressed her.

"Sorry, did you say she's an oracle?" Jason again swept his gaze over the petite girl with a riot of black curly hair. Not exactly what he'd expect of an oracle.

"She's right here. And about to—"

"Myrine, sweetheart, give the lad a break. He's had a rough couple of days. And yes, she's the best oracle this side of Delphi. She's got a way with the Fates, which you need more than anything right about now."

Jason's patience had reached the limit for Olympian smooth-talking gods with an agenda. "Maybe I do need help, eventually. But I've to get back to the island first and make things right." His emotions ripped and tore at him, needing to be with Medusa and reassure her. Except he had trust issues with Eros that kept him from buying into the whole love-god deal.

"Look at that, Myrine. True love!" Eros announced, sweeping an arm grandly toward Jason. "It consumes, inspires, and makes idiots out of the most intelligent of mortals."

That was the second time Jason had been insulted, and a bellowing rebellion against the whole Greek pantheon chafed at his already brittle patience. A pounding head and body that had seen better days was the only thing that stopped him from hightailing it out of the clinic. Well, also the lack of clothing combined with a tiny thread of manners his mother instilled about not flashing young women.

For her part, Myrine's disinterested glance made clear she didn't care what he did, naked or not. He had doubts she could offer him any help. And he wasn't even sure he wanted another mythological power mucking about in his life.

"Look, I appreciate the help, and I'm sure Myrine's an ace oracle—"

"Ace? I'm *the* oracle, English. The only decent one you'll find in this part of the world. Not that you'd be able to find one without help."

Jason gritted his teeth at her acerbic tone and how she turned to Eros, dismissing him.

"Valentine, this one is more your area than mine. I don't do love, much less take attitude from a clueless tourist," Myrine pointed out, toying with a silver tinkling charm bracelet.

It was the kind with bells Jason found utterly annoying when his students wore them in class. Another sign Myrine might not be the right oracle for the job.

"Good we're in agreement—" He tried to reason, his bare feet hitting the cool tile floor as he focused on breathing and not groaning. Not in front of the girl. He still had some dignity despite the hospital gown.

"The only thing we're in agreement about is you're being a prat and I should just leave you to fail. Which you will without us," Eros lectured.

"Ya know, I've got better things to do." Myrine shifted the bag on her shoulder, eyeing the door. Jason had a similar idea. If he could get his stiff muscles to move.

Eros sighed dramatically and tipped his head back, groaning. "Mortals." Then he faced the oracle. "Look, Myrine, I agree he's not the most worthy. And he's annoying, not the best looking, or my type."

Jason's patience shattered into Medusa's hero dust, and a plan for escape formed. "No, I'm Medusa's type. Which is who I need to be getting back to. Thanks for seeing me stitched up." He held his head high even as the gown gaped over his backside.

"See, he's consistent and determined." Eros inclined his head. "Give him a chance. He's up for the challenge even if a bit of a mess."

Jason steadied his bound shoulder and made it halfway to the door as the oracle stormed toward Eros.

"Yeah, I get it all right. The hot god needs this match to work, or he loses cred with his mother."

"This isn't about me this time, Myrine," Eros

continued, towering over the oracle. "And don't bloody think my ego didn't take a hit with these two finding true love on their own."

Just as Jason reached the door, an orderly walked in and shoved a bundle of clothing at him. He took one look at Eros and Myrine before backing out of the room.

At least he had pants.

"You wouldn't get far without those. Now if we can all agree, let's bloody get past the theatrics," Eros insisted, arching a brow at Jason's semi-bare state.

Grumbling, Jason gave up all pretense of modesty or respecting anyone else in his room, tugging off his hospital gown. Myrine seemed more invested in Eros who enthusiastically continued and perhaps enjoyed the audience a little too much.

"See, he can follow directions. And oozes sacrifice so much he ignored warnings and any sense of self-preservation to prove it to the world. I mean, mortals don't just swan in and shag a gorgon."

"Please stop." If Jason hadn't already lost any sense of decorum as he bared his ass for all to see struggling to pull on jeans one-handed, he certainly did over discussion of his sex life. Fumbling with one hand, he somehow managed to pull jeans up past his hips.

"Ugh, I did not need to see that!" Myrine said, enunciating in a Greek accent dripping with disdain.

"I dunno," Eros drew out. "A little English arse never hurt anyone. And you've gotta admit your curiosity's piqued with this one."

Ignoring the commentary, Jason tugged, hopped, and zipped up his jeans before contemplating whether he should attempt the shirt or toss it and make his escape.

"Fucking useless mortals," Eros muttered before he

roughly helped Jason into his shirt, half buttoned and hanging off his bandaged shoulder. Myrine rolled her eyes and ran a hand through thick curls held away from her face by a white band.

Cranky and edging on that queasy gonna-pass-out sensation, he kept his bare feet planted on the ground and faced Eros and his oracle. This tug of war of his choices and Medusa needed to be set straight. "You seem to be missing I made a choice long before I found this island or her. I had a plan where this trip would lead me."

"I very much doubt that," Myrine retorted. "Clearly, you need help. A nice request or a petition for me to hear your case would help."

"That's just it. I wouldn't be petitioning for just me." Jason made an attempt at a calm explanation. "This is about two of us, one of whom has lived her life at the whim of others. If I accept this favor or petition the Fates, it's like I'm making that choice for her. I need to talk to her first."

"Save me from stubborn, pig-headed mortals." Eros crossed his arms, taking up even more space in the room, which Jason admitted was a neat trick and very Olympian.

"You can't go back to that island or have a life with her as things stand. You need Myrine's help, to plead your case and win over the Fates who have more than a little pull with Olympus. You've violated Athena's temple three times and lived. You're out of whatever luck you had. I told you I need you to make a choice. This is it. So say pretty please to the nice oracle, and maybe she'll agree to help. Or tell me you're done, and you can slog off in a misery for the rest of your life."

Myrine didn't comment but gave him an unnerving

stare that left a clammy feeling crawling up his neck.

He shook it off and stood his ground. "My choice is to talk to Medusa first. You'll get your answer after I hear what she wants."

"I don't have time for idiots on suicide missions, no matter how much I approve of asking his woman first. You got bonus points for that, English." Myrine enunciated each syllable like an insult. "I've got people with bigger problems than this. Like sick kids, fishermen who need me to bless their fleet so they can feed their families and not die in a storm."

"This one's worth it even if he's in denial. This isn't casual love. He wouldn't be this stupid if it wasn't a love with enough potential and power to overcome an Olympian curse. Think of the accolades you'll get." Eros had a light in his eyes that shone with immortal power.

"Think of all Olympus coming at me, you mean," Myrine hurled back.

Tired and with his head throbbing, Jason had had enough. As they argued, he grabbed his wallet off the table next to his bed and slipped out of the room. With a slight limp, stiff movements, and exhaustion weighing down his limbs, he trudged down the hall, nodding at a nurse who stared at him before calling out for him to stop.

He ignored her and quickened his pace, sweat beading even against the cooled air. Logic and common sense be damned, he needed to do this on his own for now. Medusa would blame herself, and that pounded in his head beyond the shock, pain, or blood loss. A few days ago, jaded and bitter, he would have scoffed at the thought of loving so fiercely one could feel the pain of a lover.

Eros appeared in the blink of an eye, an irate blonde roadblock. "A less benevolent god would let you suffer in your romantic delusions. What do you think's going to happen? That Charon's going to haul your wounded arse back to that island? That Poseidon won't take you and give Charon his due? How would that make her feel? She's already given you up to keep you safe. Gods, you two are a pair. And ruining my great triumph."

"This isn't about you," Jason tightly responded with every bit of anger boiling over. "It's about her. And me, how I've—" Frustration seared through him, competing with every ache and raw nerve.

"But it is about you. You fucked up on that island, got in the way, and hurt her worse than she's been in millennia," Eros finished. "And this screw up is not the first. Here's you still running away."

"Not from her." Iron-like conviction steeled his voice. "I admit I've pushed people away. Played the bachelor hermit, used to being on my own. This is the first time I don't want that. I'm putting a relationship and her feelings first."

"Bollocks. Oh, you love her, and no doubt, you care about protecting her interests. But you're obsessed with control and running away from the one way to overcome a curse that will forever be an unsurmountable wall. Until you finally let go, feel your way through this, break down that control, and trust. It won't be easy, and you—" He poked Jason in the chest like a hot poker exploding inside his body until he gasped for air. "—will pay a price. Not her. She's paid hers, and that's why I'm still here and not off to Marbella for admittedly shallow love but enough to give me a nice buzz."

Jason rubbed at his chest with his good hand. "You

want me to do this based on altruistic faith in love? To cut some dodgy favor arrangement with deities and immortals who are well known to twist things up for their own amusement?"

"Now you're getting it!" Eros said, amusement lilting in his voice once again. "The results are all about how much you put into it, giving me and my kind sufficient faith and tribute. Of course, you have to pass a few tests to prove your worthiness, but it's not like you didn't win over a gorgon. Should be easy compared to that."

There it was. The essence of the mythology he'd studied and admired. Except, if he'd proven anything on this trip, he was a rubbish hero and an even worse expert in his field of study. He'd romanticized too much, treating everything like a bloody romantic quest instead of the gritty reality of human flaws and ruined lives.

A few days ago, he would have plunged in with no second thoughts. Now he wanted not just to live, but to have a second chance with Medusa and perhaps earn redemption for his failings.

"All right." Jason sucked in a deep breath and nodded. "Not much one for faith but for her I'll give it a go. But there's a condition."

"I don't do conditions." Eros tilted his chin and gave Jason the essence that was godly arrogance.

"Medusa isn't hurt, punished, or made to suffer more misery, no matter the outcome of whatever hell you put me through."

Eros let loose rolling laughter, like music that leached much of Jason's outrage and stress.

"Done!" Eros clamped a hand on his good shoulder and propelled him forward as life resumed around them.

"First things first. You reek worse than a centaur, and you could use a posh up. Can't plead your case looking like this. We have standards, you know."

"Standards," Jason grumpily muttered, allowing himself to be led from the small hospital into the bright sun, nearly blinding him. Symbolic, maybe. Uneasiness slowed his pace. This could go terribly wrong.

Eros had gotten it right. Things were spinning out of his control. Being forced to trust in mercurial Olympians made his stomach knot up and rebel. The only person he felt ironclad trust for was the one person he couldn't run to.

"Come along back there! We've got places to be," Eros called out, way too chipper.

"This is going to be a complete cock-up." As if to prove his point, he stubbed a toe on a loose rock on the rutted dirt street. "He gives me clothes but no shoes. This doesn't bode well."

Chapter Fourteen

"This round's on me!" Eros' voice rang out after he shoved Jason into the bar. Several people raised their glasses *to Valentine*. Eros nodded, preening before he guided Jason toward the stairs. "Not you, petitioner. Off you go to get presentable. And make sure you look better than Cerberus' chew toy."

Jason stewed and grumbled as he trudged up the stairs. He slammed the door to his room as he sucked in air at the stomach-clenching pain burning in his shoulder.

"Posh up, be a good petitioner. Bollocks," he grumbled, ducking into the tiny bathroom, and flinched at the reflection in the mirror.

"Been shot. What did he expect?" He turned on the creaking faucet, letting the water splash against his fingers. Days ago he was washing up in Medusa's temple. How quickly life changed.

Not unlike he told Eros how he'd changed. Jason wanted more from life. More time with Medusa, to wake up every morning with her, relaxed and connected to someone he loved. That's why he needed the oracle. Even if he had to play nice and follow the rules for whatever a petitioner needed to do.

He filled the sink and grunted as he undressed. Pain medication long gone, he struggled through a sponge bath and grooming until he looked, as Eros had insisted, like a man Medusa might not toss out of her temple. And he knew what that felt like. Not that he would tell Eros the details of that day.

He managed jeans, a button up, and even a splash of cologne. Leaning toward the small square mirror, he rubbed his good hand across his now clean-shaven jaw.

"Not bad. At least for a meeting with an oracle."

When he jostled his injured shoulder, he winced, and his thoughts turned back to the madness of relying on an oracle or the legendary Fates to solve his problems. Although his inner academic vibrated with excitement at once again proving his theories correct.

Except he couldn't ignore that slightly acerbic critical voice that sounded remarkably like his brother. Oracles and the Fates didn't do free favors. A price was always levied and often in unexpected ways.

The sodding fine print would no doubt bite him in the arse. Even thousands of years ago, they'd had bureaucratic ways of sticking it to the unsuspecting.

Still cradling his arm, he paced the cramped room. Pressure mounted, pounding in the back of his head. They'd want payment, an offering, and he needed to outthink whatever they demanded. He wasn't risking just his arse this time.

Eros had made a big deal over sacrifice. Getting shot had been more his stupidity and overconfidence than falling on his proverbial sword. Was staying with her sacrifice? It didn't feel that way. Maybe he could offer up his freedom as a trade before leaving his unfulfilling life behind. It wasn't like he'd planned to go back. Although he'd miss libraries, a decent curry, coffee, and a cold beer.

"She's worth it." Vocalizing his decision, no matter

where it might lead, seemed to get his arse in gear.

If Eros and the Fates wanted a sacrifice or grand gesture, surrendering his freedom should tick a few boxes. He quickly grabbed his messenger bag and took one last look in the mirror. With a touch of swagger and confidence, he marched down the stairs and toward destiny.

He ignored the sudden silence in the bar.

Eros' favorite waitress, Petra, shoved a crumpled paper at him. "From Valentine."

"Thanks." He glanced at the scrawling writing and directions.

Petra gave him one more of her narrowed looks before turning back to her customers. At least, the mistrust-the-foreigner attitude didn't change. Kind of comforting and somewhat normal. Or whatever normal was for him now.

The late-evening heat and humidity slammed against him as he left the inn. It dragged at his feet on the hard-packed dirt road, not unlike the exhaustion from a throbbing shoulder. He passed a few people, none of whom paid him any mind. Which was the way he liked it.

Once he translated the ornate, looping writing, the instructions were simple. One block past the corner market, he turned toward a single-story café, Mystra. Odd place for an oracle but then he'd gotten it wrong from so many historical accounts. He couldn't entirely trust what he'd thought he knew before arriving on the island seven days ago.

Pungent scents of garlic, oregano, and roasted meats greeted him inside the dimly lit café packed with patrons enjoying an early meal.

"Walker?" He was greeted by a frowning hostess in a plain black dress, gray hair tied back in a knot.

"Valentine sent me," he acknowledged with Eros' alias.

The woman squinted her eyes and gave him a once-over before issuing a terse, "Follow."

He squeezed in between patrons who paused conversations to watch him duck under low-hanging lanterns and cradle his shoulder covered by an untucked white dress shirt.

Through a black-curtained doorway, he stepped into the kitchen. He passed cooks who gave him a similar examination. Bloody brilliant. Everyone in the small community apparently knew or had an inkling he'd mucked up their secret about Medusa.

He mentally repeated she was worth a little discomfort. A few annoyed locals he could handle. Even the oracle didn't put him off. History and mythology were his element. Even if he might have a few of the details wrong.

He ducked past another black curtain into a storage closet where Valentine sat on a wooden stool, sipping wine. Legs stretched out, he appeared unconcerned and chatted up a buxom redhead fetching bottles of wine. She laughed until her gaze landed on Jason. Then her smile slipped into a tight-lipped mask.

"Are you gonna stand there gaping or get to it?" Myrine sat on the floor cross-legged.

He hated how flustered he felt and not just startled by Myrine's demanding attitude. Eros always seemed to capture his attention in any room, causing his skin to heat and that damnable heart-pumping jolt that should be saved for something other than godly glamour. Of course all that went out the window when Myrine's dark eyes bored into him. His chest grew tight, and chills raced down his back under her probing gaze. If he had doubt about her, it had long fled. She was way more than the rebellious teenager she appeared to be.

"I'm apologizing now for not knowing the proper etiquette. It's been a while since I read about the Pythia and such." He slowly, and a little painfully, sank to the floor, cross-legged, opposite her. A few joints might have popped, much to his annoyance.

She snorted and held out her hand, palm up.

"She doesn't do this for free, mate," Eros said, entirely too happy.

"Right, and payment would be?" He reached into his back pocket. Pain knifed through his shoulder until he felt his stomach curdle. This was going so well.

"Everything you got. No credit cards or checks."

A sudden amusement lightened the mood as he slid out his wallet. The powers that be didn't take bank cards. "Traveler's checks?" he asked, offering up his billfold.

"Gods, but you're work. I've already made an exception for you, English, so yeah, take advantage of the oracle," she snapped before snatching his wallet and emptying the contents on the floor between them. She paused to look at the picture of his parents.

"They're at peace." She gently tucked the picture into the black leather billfold before she tossed the wallet back at him. "You're not and haven't been for a long while. Maybe that's why she likes you." She scooped up the pile of bills, traveler's checks, and coins and dropped her fee into a basket before leveling another piercing stare at him.

"Well?" He shifted uncomfortably under her

scrutiny and readjusted his bound arm.

She remained silent, tapping pink-painted nails on her black leggings before giving him a long drawn-out sigh.

He bristled, wondering why he had to get the young, cheeky oracle. Best get to the point. "I'm here to ask your help. I went to see Medusa to prove my work even if it ended me," he admitted, his voice growing rough. "When she didn't kill me right off, it knocked the academic attitude out of me. I—"

"My Gods!" She groaned, crossing her arms. "Save me from the chattering English boomer. Can you just get to the point? I've got two more behind you."

"Not a boomer," he snapped. "At least get your generational insults right." He stopped as she made a production of looking at the watch on her wrist. "Fine, I love Medusa and want to spend my life with her. Hopefully, all in one piece. I'm asking you, Myrine, to remind the Fates of all Medusa has done, protecting Athena's temple, enduring the loneliness, taking lives as she was charged, and suffering unbearable pain at each life she took. She's served Athena faithfully. I don't want to disrespect the goddess. I'm asking her to allow me to spend my mortal years with Medusa. I'll leave my world and my freedom behind for her. It would be nice if I could do that without dying a horrible death. It's not like the Olympians didn't already take my parents."

Maybe that was a little too far. Fuck if he knew how far was too far. Even with all his research and knowledge. And he was humbled by having to admit he might be out of his league.

Silence sat heavy in the air. No one said a word or acknowledged anything.

The teenager leaned back and cocked her head, staring at him. "They took your parents?" she asked and pulled out a purple silken pouch and proceeded to dump the contents on the tiled floor between them.

"No way, are those bones?" he asked, sweeping aside the angry knot in his stomach for the excitement at the real-world application of things he'd only read about.

"Yes, now be quiet. You've got a lot to unpack." She poked at shards of thin and jagged dirty white bone fragments.

He was ten seconds away from reaching for one.

"No touching. You be a good petitioner and sit still." Her brow pinched, and her fingers clawed into her knees before she sat back and stared across the room.

He hated to admit it, but he leaned forward in anticipation, grunting once at the ache in his shoulder.

"I need a moment." She dismissed him with a wave of her hand and pulled out her cell phone and slipped in earbuds. Her eyes slipped shut, and she sat passively.

He was the opposite of passive. He fidgeted, tapping fingers on his knee, tension winding up so tight he thought he might snap. He didn't like being played or at the mercy of forces with a history of tormenting people. These Fates had snipped off the lives of his parents. They'd sat idle when Medusa had been unfairly cursed.

What if this failed? No, even if they rejected his request, he'd find another way. His heart clenched, and a dull ache sank deep into his chest. He'd never felt so deeply for another person. This petitioning, waiting, and not doing drove him barmy.

"Easy, my lad. I feel the heartbreak all the way over here. This isn't personal. It's how she works," Eros spoke after the extended silence.

Jason snorted, and before he could hurl a sarcastic remark on how bloody personal it was for him, Myrine spoke.

"You need to check your attitude." Her eyes opened, and she removed the earbuds, dark eyes casting a laser-like intensity, slicing through him.

"I've used that same line on my students," he admitted, and it hit him. Teacher, student. Oracle and petitioner. Oh, how the tables had turned. "Not that you're—"

"No, I'm not. Neither are you anymore. If you ever were. You, Jason Walker, have been coasting, never living or connecting to people, your brother, your students, friends, or lovers. That's your problem. You think you know everything, think that you know your place in all this." She waved a hand in the air around the room and barked a hard laugh. "The only thing you got right is loving her and coming to me. No offense to Valentine." She inclined her head at Eros.

"None taken. Until the happily ever after, that is. Then I expect loads of credit."

"For your favor." Jason didn't want to say that phrase, but it popped out.

"Exactly! See, Myrine, he's starting to see."

"Maybe," she drew out, again giving him a once-over. "But he has to prove it. The one truth in this mortal realm is if you want something, you gotta pay."

"I did. You took everything in my wallet." Righteous indignation stiffened his spine, and he flushed hot from all the waiting and insults.

"That was nothing. A consultation fee. I'm talking about sacrifice, faith, and tribute. You're the big expert and read all the books. You didn't just come for a reading of your fate. You're asking for intervention and a good word whispered in the right places. I mean, why should they help you, who has never prayed to anyone or anything? It's time to man up and make a real sacrifice, not just play the hero, but be it."

Jason had been challenged many times in his life, by his brother and colleagues and even a one-off girlfriend. He could argue and cite his accomplishments, published works, and contributions. But she was talking about more than academics or accomplishments. Fear tempered his ego, and dark thoughts about failing Medusa stole even more of his confidence.

"I'm not going to deny my failings or how I lived my life. All I know is that meeting Medusa, being with her, is the first time I wanted to be with someone and not push her away. Maybe it doesn't make sense. It's not like I understand it. I just know what I feel, and not being with her isn't an option for me. My mum, she always told me when I met the one, I'd know. It wouldn't be all sex and fiery passion, although can't deny that."

"Please, I don't need gory details." Myrine shuddered in dramatic fashion.

"Passion isn't gory. Or if it is, then you're doing it wrong." He tried to rein in the scowl and oncoming lecture on sexuality and repression of feminine power. That's not why he was there. "I'm trying to explain this isn't a lark or me studying her for an academic paper. What's between us defies reason. I don't have to feel guarded with her, and her happiness, it...oh blimey." He rubbed at the corner of his eye. "It's like a light going off on the inside. I don't do grand romance other than reading the classics for my work. Now I get bloody dopey happy from just hearing her giggle. Her happiness is worth more than any degree, peer review, or published paper. So I don't know what these Fates want of me, but it's worth it if I can make her smile, even locked in that temple away from the rest of the world."

Saying the words out loud, admitting his feelings, stunned him to the point he squirmed like he hadn't since his mum caught him in a study session mid-snog with Kalinda Patel.

"Now I understand why Valentine brought you and why *they* knew your name so well." A smile curved her lips, and she nodded.

"The Fates know me by name?" He spoke slowly, a shiver streaking through him at the thought of why such powerful beings had an eye on him.

"I give you a fifty-fifty chance of making this work. You'll go back to your room, get some rest, meditate, try and get your spirit calmed down because, man, you are whacked out. You'll get instructions in the morning. Read them, and no googling shit. They hate that. You've got to go with your gut. That's part of this. Everything must be done by sunset. This'll end one of two ways. You love her or you die. Either she gets you or Hades does."

His head spun, and he focused on breathing. This was real in a way his first half-cocked plan to prove Medusa hadn't been. Mortality hadn't really sunk in.

"Excellent!" Valentine exclaimed and stood, holding a hand out to Jason.

Jason looked at Myrine, who seemed a little too pleased, standing up and brushing herself off. Too late to regret choosing this path. He accepted Valentine's hand and the tug upward.

"Now the real work starts. Let's get you back to the

inn." Eros slapped him on his good shoulder, and he looked back at Myrine once more. She'd lost the sulking teen vibe and had an air of tranquility settling over her.

"Thank you for your help."

"You may not feel that way tomorrow," she warned. "But if it means anything, I hope you succeed and find happiness with her. She deserves that."

Jason stumbled back a step as Valentine shoved him toward the exit. In a daze, he walked through the curtained door, barely seeing the kitchen or diners. Outside, the oppressive heat of the day had turned into an evening chill that quickly seeped beneath his shirt. He stopped long enough to take in the stars and mentally said a prayer. Myrine accused him of not believing in anything. He did believe in his parents and a universe that seemed fickle. After meeting with her, he felt a compulsion to make a prayer to whatever deity listened, and maybe to his parents, hoping they'd be with him one last time.

Chapter Fifteen

Medusa kicked a clay amphora out of her way as she chewed a thumbnail, pacing the temple. Night had fallen, and she wrapped herself in Jason's coat. Earlier, she'd tried to erase his presence from the temple and stop her torment. It was useless. His ghost, the essence of him, seemed embedded in every crack and crevice.

Every time she saw the screaming statue of the girl who'd shot him, she sank into a mixture of seething anger and loss. Eventually, she'd smashed the statue until it was rubble. Not that it brought her anything other than bloodied knuckles.

Her respite was in paging through his sketchbook or burying her face in his leftover clothing. The heaviness of grief constricting around her was so wrong. She should be happy he lived and was back in his own world. Emotions couldn't be so neatly tucked away. Even her snakes hissed and writhed in discontent until her scalp itched.

Ever since Eros visited, she'd gone mad with worry. What if others were interfering in Jason's life? It had been two days since she ordered Charon to take him to safety. Her imagination went wild with all the ways Jason could be harmed or worse. Though a tiny sliver of hope still lingered.

After all, her stubborn Jason didn't give up on her the first time. Even ordering Charon to avoid his charge of delivering victims to her was a delay tactic. If she was sure of anything, Jason had the tenacity of Cerberus on the trail of an escaped soul. And then there was Eros out for glory.

Too many questions and possible ways for Jason to suffer haunted her. Her temple practically swelled with the biggest question of them all. What forces, Olympian or otherwise, manipulated Jason? It festered deep in her belly until she'd paced ruts in the mosaic floors.

Eros only cared about winning, proving a point to Olympus, and, in a typically twisted way, making it all about him. She doubted he'd risk pissing off Athena or raising the ire of Zeus. No one wanted that. Ever.

She found Jason's coat amidst the rubble of her anger. Another reminder of how he'd left pieces of himself behind. Barely able to swallow her grief, she scooped it up and pulled the coat tight around her shoulders. The clean woodsy scent only tore further into her emotional wounds, prompting her to continue the circuit of her temple. Until she stopped dead still and spun around near the crumbled remains of a former victim.

"The blindfold. The Fates." Her snakes grew silent, and the light filtering into the temple dimmed as clouds drifted across the moon. Only the burning braziers flickered against the darkness. Fear crept though the temple, her fear this time.

"Eros is working with the Fates or, worse, using them to even a score on Olympus and gain his own glory." There it was, one of the most dangerous paths Jason might take. She swallowed hard and collapsed onto a stone bench, scrubbing at her face. He'd said he loved her, and she'd felt that love warming the cold places in her temple. Love made fools of mortals and gods alike.

Her emotions whipped and snapped as much as her snakes as they cursed the foolish who trespassed in her temple. Except Jason. Proof positive Medusa, daughter of Phorcys and Ceto, didn't allow her curse to control her. She'd told Eros she had influence beyond this temple, and that wasn't an exaggeration. Invigorated and bursting with determination, she launched from her bench, a gorgon on a mission.

"They think I'll sit here, cowering and helpless." Fury coursed through her like the flames of Tartarus. She marched over to her alcove, swept aside the curtains, and tore through her ancient hinged chest containing the few things she kept tucked away for herself. Like Jason's sketchbook.

This time, she was not a soppy mess reminiscing and pining. She shrugged off the coat, then flung it onto her bed. A gorgon on a mission, she shoved aside cloaks and goblets, then grabbed a black-glazed oil lantern. She tucked the unadorned flat-design lamp under her arm and grabbed a carafe of oil and an old gold-corded tie for her gown. With her arms full, she made her way to the flaming brazier.

It had been centuries since she observed the old ceremonies. She carefully filled the oil lamp and set it aside. She cut the cord with a ceremonial knife once used for sacrifice to Athena and soaked the cord in the oil. Sacrifice was what had brought her to this point, only it had been Jason's for her. In his name, she said a fervent prayer to her family and the one god who could give her answers. She lit the lamp, a relic now, but in its day, a sacred item forged in honor of the one she summoned.

Annoyingly, it took a while to burn.

She heaved a sigh and plopped it on the floor and sat cross-legged. "I know you don't like being called like this. You're the only one who can tell me what's really going on and not to curry favor. And you owe me."

The flame flared, and the sea breeze whisked through the temple, tearing at the flames in the brazier and fluttering her curtains.

"Noble Hermes, I call upon you to deliver to me that which I need to know."

The wind died down. Her mood plummeted. No Hermes. Just one pathetic lamp flickering and spitting oil.

"Are you going to make me scream at the ocean and unleash my inner gorgon on unsuspecting birds and fish?"

"What in Hades is your problem?" The masculine voice echoed in her temple. The lilting accent similar to Jason's resonated with a wash of power across her skin.

Medusa didn't turn her gaze away from the flame although relief and a tiny spark of amusement relaxed her tense shoulders.

"My problem is Eros and the Fates possibly killing the man I love for their own sick pleasure. And that's just for starters. I need to know what's happening out there. Something is brewing. I can feel it even in the dank air of my temple. It's slithering in the dark, the question of who's playing games with his life and mine."

She caught a glimpse of the blur of silver armor and ebony limbs of the Olympian messenger. He kept his distance, but she'd seen enough of him to understand why he'd made the rounds with nymphs and goddesses. Tall, muscular, dimpled cheeks on a strong jaw combined with a cascade of midnight-black braids, he gave plenty of mortals and gods alike wet dreams.

"I've had my fill of illicit love affairs." He groaned. "You heard about Seph and Hades?"

"Yes, she's married and a queen with a husband who adores her."

"Her mum nearly destroyed all the mortal realms. Not to mention, yours truly had to deliver the news of how her daughter was off doing Hades. I don't need to get in the middle of any more forbidden shagging couples."

"Oh please!" Medusa's temper flared, and she stood, warming her hands over the open flames of the brazier. "You've seduced enough of Olympus and mortals to complain about one couple who at least found some form of happiness. All I'm asking for is gossip on one mortal, Jason Walker. And who is showing an interest in him and anything you know about what Eros is up to."

She heard him fluttering around the rafters before the clink of his armor sounded behind a column.

"You took a mortal as a lover? I mean, how does that work with you being cursed and all?"

"I didn't ask you here to talk about my sex life." She flushed hot and nearly pummeled a nearby statue at even uttering those words. Of course, the positive was she now had a sex life to be protective of.

"Quid pro quo, Gorgon. If I give you salacious Olympian dirt, you need to spill the tea on how you ended up with a mortal and what that smart-arsed love god has to do with it. He's been missing from the last few of Aphrodite's festivals. She's been a right terror about it."

Her snakes hissed and writhed in an anxiety

matching hers. Pissed-off goddesses ended in curses or death. She had to get a grip or convince Hermes to use that hot-messenger-god charm to distract Olympus from looking too hard at Eros. Of course, the fact that she was now covering for Eros chafed her very fine gorgon ass.

"Eros says he's been drawn here, to Jason and—" She didn't want to reveal too much. "You know how he is. He gets a kick out of impossible lovers and suffering for love. It's making my snakes have anxiety." Not quite the truth but she wasn't about to tell him that her snakes loved Jason too.

"That sounds about right. So this mortal bloke is going mad, then?"

"No! At least I hope not. He's the first mortal to come here and not, you know, try to kill me. He's a scholar, and I sent him away to live his life. But he loves me now, and Eros is up to something. I'm worried it could be more than Eros involved. I need to know who and what."

"Gods, why do I get dragged into these things?" He moaned.

"You're not dragged into anything," she emphasized, thinking of how to not look too pathetic and get her point across. "This is about information, and no onc knows the Fates and Olympus like you do. So you've not heard Jason's name mentioned or anything about the Fates giving favor to a mortal?"

"The Fates. Bloody Tartarus, this is deep. Lucky for you, I happened to be enjoying a few glasses of some of Seph's finest ambrosia with Dionysus. He might have confided that one of his devotees heard that the Fates were bored, and their favorite oracle offered up a chance to get back at Aphrodite for pitching a fit over the untimely death of her favorite mortal lover."

Medusa snorted and circled the fire, worries building at perverted godly vendettas, and didn't she know a few things about those? "And?" she probed.

"If I'm getting this right, your mortal is in the thick of this. Not a good place to be. Not a good place for any of us. Especially if it pits Eros against his mum in some twisted family feud."

"Yes, I know that!" she snapped at him as urges to unleash her curse rose to the surface, not that it would solve anything, which was the only thing that reined in the power racing across her skin.

"Sorry," she quickly tacked on.

"Sorry's not going to do you any good. Me either."

"Is there anything I can do?" Helplessness seeped around her.

"You really love this mortal?"

"If I say yes, he'll be condemned. If I say no, some other horrible thing will happen to him for daring to love me."

"Gods, but you've got it bad. Not that the last two thousand years were a joyride, but at least here you're safe away from Olympian backstabbing and the heartbreak that comes from love."

"My heart is already breaking." Her throat ached to admit the pain that raked through her like she was being ripped apart. "I can endure it if I knew Jason was safe from interfering Olympians with grudges and petulant rivalries."

"Good luck with that. You know how things are. And this love thing, a lot of that is about letting go and trust. If he's gone to the Fates, there's nothing anyone can do but him. Not even Eros can change their decision.

You know how powerful choice is."

Gods, did she. Her choice led her to an eternity in this temple. But she'd also chosen to spare Jason. "If he finds favor with the Fates and Eros gives his blessing as well, things could still end badly. There's still Athena and Aphrodite who could go to Zeus. He could—"

"Go down in flames and then to Hades, which wouldn't be such a bad thing. Hades is as fair as you get on Olympus and pretty happy down there when his wife is home," Hermes acknowledged with far too much levity.

His nonchalant attitude irked her that he took things so lightly. She focused on not hurling him out like she had Jason that first day. Not that it stopped Jason and it would only piss off Hermes. She needed allies more than venting.

"The point is I don't want Jason to die or be judged in the Underworld."

"Might not go that way. We are talking impossible love. That'd earn Eros major bonus points, which I'm guessing he's going to use as redemption to make up for all the crap he's pulled." Hermes seemed to be thinking this through now and not just brushing it off. "Like the whole thing with Apollo. Course, Aphrodite will have another tantrum at Eros achieving something she never did or even tried. Hera will eat that up and use it in whatever plans she's up to. Athena will get something out of it because you know she still holds a grudge. And your mortal, who knows. He's out of his league. That's all I got."

Exhaustion weighed her down. Too much Olympian drama always did. Now all she had was prayer and temple duty. But hope still lingered. Her Jason might not be a warrior, but he was clever and true of heart.

"Thank you, Hermes. I don't suppose I could ask you not to pass this around. At least not until Jason's fate is decided."

He groaned, and she heard his boots stomp toward the balcony.

"Only because you're one of my favorites."

"And you don't want to get on the Fates' bad side or have a couple of unhappy goddesses toss you across all the mortal realms," she teased, although with a waning lightness. "I know this might have been a risk. Thank you again for coming and being honest."

"Maybe next delivery, I'll have good news or, you know, make a delivery for two."

Medusa listened to him leave her temple in a gust of air. She didn't dare hope for what Hermes had spoken of. Centuries of disappointment and regrets taught her that to wish too hard for a thing made it more painful when it didn't happen. She dragged her feet back to bed and curled up in her blankets and Jason's coat.

"Please don't do anything foolish," she wished and prayed to Jason before sleep finally claimed her.

Chapter Sixteen

Dreams kept Jason from rest.

He stood on a beach in the midst of a storm, his bare feet sunken into wet sand. His mum waded in hip-deep water, jeans and oxford-blue shirt plastered to her thin frame. Enormous waves crashed around both of them, but she didn't flinch. She never did against anyone or anything. Always throwing her shoulders back, she met challenges with eyes that matched his.

Only this time, a sad smile lifted against high cheekbones before she gave him a nod. The wind howled, ripping at her long gray hair. Rain stung his skin as he shouted for her. Behind him, Medusa's voice called out, beckoning him to be safe.

He jerked awake, his legs twisted in the covers and heart racing. Voices drifted through the plank wooden floor, a weirdly comforting sound. He inched up to sitting and breathed through the last of his nightmare. Twinges and itching pain irritated his shoulder until he let loose a few curses. Until he noticed a parchment scroll, sitting oh so innocently on a blue velvet pillow at the foot of his bed.

Days and weeks ago, excitement would have pounded in him for the discovery and intrigue, propelling him to sweep it up and study every detail. Now, however, after a brush with the brutal reality of Medusa's life and how he'd had his arse kicked from his failure at the whole hero role, Jason admitted he needed to take a moment and think before acting. Especially facing what could be a scroll of doom.

But he'd asked for this. Pleaded his case with the oracle. Now the first step toward winning the favor of the Fates sat on his bed. A twinge of doubt twisted in his gut. The whole idea of a test or journey of faith could end in death or worse. Given his track record of late and the lashing the oracle had given him, he'd be lucky if he survived walking out the door.

"It's just a scroll," he muttered, tossing off the blankets and stretching as he stomped naked around the bed. "Or I'm still in a hospital, drugged out of my mind." He snorted and poked at the bandages binding his shoulder and arm. The very real bullet wound throbbed into a dull ache. Yeah, that felt real enough.

He stopped at the end of the bed, and his hand hovered over the parchment until he thought about Medusa. She'd said he wouldn't survive in her home realm. His failure at keeping her safe and at all the things he should be good at still scalded his ego.

The old morality stories about mortals and gods should've better prepared him. Then there was Medusa. Her life story and thinking about consequence gave him pause about how dangerous a scroll from the gods could be. She'd even been in his dream, warning him and…*ohhh*. The dream wasn't just guilt. He yanked his hand away.

"They were right. I'm an idiot. It's all connected." If he wasn't already injured, he might bang his head against the wall. His mum, the stormy seas, and years of dreams varying but still the same topic. He'd dismissed them as guilt for not being with his parents that day. How much of his restless nights were an ever-building warning of doom? And now Medusa was tangled up in whatever it all meant.

He should know better. He'd studied both Hesiod and Homer who wrote of dreams as messages from the divine. Or as warnings.

Now he was beginning to understand Eros' edict that he shower and clean up. The whole cleanse the mind and body concept wasn't unusual in rituals. It was time for him to start acting with more thought and less impatience and impulse. Medusa deserved that. And like Eros complained, she deserved a man who groomed as well as used his brain. He doubted the world would come to an end while he showered. Still best be cautious. He gave the scroll a wide berth.

"Don't even think it." Yes, he chastised a scroll. And he was done wasting time. First a quick and careful shower to wash away the morning brain fog and give him clarity. Then he'd deal with the scroll.

The tepid water barely eking out didn't seem to make things clearer other than aggravate him in his efforts to wash around his injury and ramp up his paranoia. Nothing could be taken at face value.

Especially his dream. He wracked his brain about the themes and symbolism. Certainly, it was about loss, choice, and possibly a reference to Poseidon who could be a player in all this. Or it was false and meant to mislead him. The water turned icy, fouling his already cranky mood. A few minutes later he nicked himself shaving.

"Blood sacrifice would just about be next. Not that I'm offering." He looked upward, hoping a good scowl would deter any mythological entity or deity from getting any ideas. Still, he saved the wadded-up tissue just in case, and wasn't that a gruesome thought? Blood sacrifice had better be off the table.

With a few choice words and curses, he managed to dress. Arse on the bed, he put on this glasses and then gently picked up the scroll and untied the blue ribbon binding it. In black loopy handwriting was a list and a deadline. Sundown that day.

"A feather of pure white, an unknown story from a stranger, a loaf of bread made by your hand, a sacrifice of vanity, and a symbol of devotion." He tightened his fingers until the thick cream paper crumpled. There it was. Symbolic, vague, and up to interpretation. This was going to be a long day.

"Oh, love, they are testing me, but you're worth it." She would disagree, and that's what fired up his resolve. He tucked away his glasses before he grabbed his wristwatch, an extra sketch pad, graphite, and his good-luck charm, a small, first-century bone carved horse missing a leg. Not that he believed in luck or magic, but then again, here he was on a quest to convince mythological deities to give him a shot with his gorgon lover. On that thought, he forged onward.

He paused on the stairs, adjusting the bag on his good shoulder, confidence building. The feather wouldn't be too difficult. Stories tended to happen over a drink or coffee. Doable. Vanity was always a biggie in myths. The bread, though, that would take some doing. He focused on the bread as he made his way down the rest of the stairs.

Eros was suspiciously missing from the dimly lit pub. A handful of people were eating early breakfast. So much for godly favor. This one was apparently on him.

"Uh, sorry to bother you, Petra." He plastered on what he hoped was a charming smile at the young woman carrying a tray of coffee who always treated him with a perpetual bitch face.

"Valentine isn't here."

"Thanks, but what I really need is a favor."

"Again?" No doubt the lady did not like him.

To be fair, he'd not made an effort to be friendly. Although he'd always made sure to leave tips even when it wasn't customary. Apparently, he hadn't quite earned favors for that.

Time to pour on the rusty-but-not-forgotten Walker family charm. After all, Medusa thought he was charming. And it was her job to kill anyone who walked into her temple. That must count for something.

"This is going to sound odd, but is there a bakery or a place I could get bread-making lessons?"

He caught a few patrons giving him a little too much attention. *Charm*, he reminded himself, offering a smile. He'd already poshed up his accent so he wouldn't sound like a lunatic, and combined with combed hair and a splash of cologne, he could smooth over any locals who might question him. Granted, with one arm in a sling, he wasn't the typical tourist and not exactly up to snuff for bread baking.

Petra snorted but cracked a smile while giving him a once-over before taking pity, he assumed.

"Agatas. Go down to the shoe store, turn right."

She swept away, dismissing him. Which was fine by him as he quickly exited the den of gossips pretending not to stare at him.

The sun already beat down, reflecting off the white buildings until he squinted. His sunglasses were with

Medusa along with a few of his other more important worldly possessions, which hopefully he would be rejoining at the end of the day. Not hopefully. He would. If anyone was up to solving a few tasks, symbolic or otherwise, it was him.

Of course, a few minutes later, he wanted to kick himself. The bakery wasn't a true bakery. It was a house. And a glaring, elderly gray-haired woman speaking loudly in Greek. Although not the best at the spoken language, he made out enough of what she said with the words *useless tourists* and an insult of his manhood.

"Yes, you're probably right." He smiled and nodded. And in what he hoped was sufficient Greek, he said, "But I need your help."

She heaved a sigh and crossed her thin arms across the loose flower-print dress, hair pulled into a severe bun.

"It's for the woman I love." He flinched and looked around the low-ceilinged entryway lined with boxes of what he assumed were baked goods.

She eyed his shoulder and let loose a few more choice words before waving him to follow her. It couldn't be that easy. Of course, it wasn't, as the Fates had a twisted sense of humor, making him earn their favor.

The kitchen was so small he had to duck to enter and bumped against crates stacked on the floor and narrowly avoided pots hanging from the ceiling.

A young boy of maybe ten in a T-shirt and shorts stoked a fire in a classic Greek clay oven on the opposite side of the room.

The woman, Toula, he learned eventually, shouted, "Luca!"

The boy gave Jason a frown before wiping his hands on a dish towel and turning toward Toula.

"The tourist wants to make the bread." She continued to watch him suspiciously as the boy tossed the dish towel on the counter.

"That's about it." Jason spoke in broken Greek. "I need a loaf by sundown…for a present." *Quick thinking, Dr. Walker, published and respected author of* The Cultural Impact of the Hellenistic Gods on Modern Society. Or perhaps not by the way the boy glared in that same way Myrine had. He never was as good with young kids as he was with his uni students, and even then, they either flirted or paid him little attention.

"Fifty thousand drachmae." The boy held his hand out.

"Er, that's a problem. You see I'm sort of low on cash…" He trailed off, nearly bonking his head on a hanging pan when he fidgeted. "You don't by chance know Myrine?"

The boy's glare turned into laughter. Toula did not laugh. A scowl etched even deeper in her aged face.

"What you got?" the boy asked, this time in English.

Bartering, he was prepared for. "You need a tutor? Help passing your exams? Books?"

The boy eyed his wristwatch.

"Fine." Jason held out his wrist for the boy to take the leather-banded watch. It was only his father's. His stomach knotted at losing another connection to his parents. The past few days seemed to carve away at that hollowed-out space he'd walled off since his parents died.

The watch was just a thing. He'd left plenty of material things behind when he came here with every intention of not surviving. And it's not like the watch kept proper time. It was worth it for Medusa. Not like he'd need a watch at the temple.

Still…he stared at how his bare wrist represented what these deities did. They cleaved and carved at the flesh, at emotions, until nothing was left but bones. Maybe that's all that was left after years of hard work. Sure, he'd helped a few students, and he'd taken satisfaction from watching them grow and succeed. In the end, nothing had been enough. Even his department head saw that, making it easy to dispose of him. Like he'd disposed of the watch.

"Are we good, then?" Jason tried to shove aside his past failings. He watched the boy affix the watch on his wrist, his slim fingers tracing the glass face.

That tight ache in his chest eased. Luca appreciated the watch more than he did. Blimey, a lifetime of lessons were being drilled into him. He cleared his throat and stretched out his hand. "You're Luca, right? I'm Jason."

One man-to-man handshake and he was dropping his bag off to the side.

And thus began his grand journey into bread making, which included copious shouting, pointing, and Luca having fun at his expense.

Flour and yeast turned into a goopy chemistry experiment called starter, and he was soon dumping it all into a bowl, mixing and kneading one-handed until he thought his hand would cramp. Flour dusted his clothes, and Jason learned a new definition of hell.

Sticky, wet dough wasn't exactly like caressing his lover. Despite what Luca kept implying. The kid shouldn't even know about that.

"Mate, if you think this is what caressing the fairer

sex feels like, you and I should have a talk." He twisted his wrist to push and pull more of the sticky mess, which Luca assured would turn into a crusty bread.

"Love is patience. Dough needs to be smooth," Luca lectured as Toula smacked his hand with a sharp, "*Enough!*"

He suspected she knew more English than she let on. Luca pointed toward the sink where he washed up while Toula draped linen over his and three other bowls she'd made while he struggled with his one. At least he was able to one-handed catch the linen cloth Lucas tossed. He still had skills, just not the bread-making kind.

"Now we peel," Luca informed him, pulling out a sack of oranges and two large wooden bowls.

"Right," Jason muttered, following his bread-making instructor outside.

They sat on wooden stools outside the hot, cramped kitchen as the sea breeze swept through the trees that shaded the narrow back garden. Luca divided peel from the orange slices in two bowls. Two goats watched them while eating grass.

And what philosophical lesson was he expected to learn next? How to charm goats?

"So what are we making?" Jason tried to ignore the goats that looked a little too interested in his untucked shirt. He shifted uncomfortably as his thoughts turned to gods masquerading as animals and how that never ended well for unsuspecting mortals.

"For the jam. We peel while dough rises."

Jason fumbled, used his knees, and generally bit back a number of curses while a simple fruit defeated him. Peeling oranges one-handed didn't exactly work out. Unless it was to amuse Luca.

"Sorry, not much of an orange peeler." He tossed the orange and caught it one-handed. "I could trade you a story. I don't suppose you have a story you've never told anyone else?" he asked.

The dark-haired boy's gray eyes sparkled with mischief. "You first." The boy had already peeled and sorted three oranges.

"Fair enough." Jason leaned against the side of the house, adjusting his sling. Most of his stories wouldn't be appropriate for a kid. Reminiscing wasn't something he did often, but maybe that was part of this task.

"When I was your age, I was a right terror. Don't know how my mum and dad survived it." That earned him a smile, and for the first time in days, he felt less guarded. Not so far as relaxed, but more at ease. Words tumbled from him, recounting his youth when he was less driven and more interested in escaping daily boredom.

"My brother liked to be the boss of me, and I liked to annoy him. Still do. But there was this time he was to be watching me, and I buggered off on my own, went to the library. Which may not sound exciting but it is when you're camped out overnight, eating crisps and biscuits, reading about wizards and subverting authority. We both were grounded, and he missed out on a date with this girl he'd been chasing after for ages. Pretty much summed up our relationship."

Luca grinned, giving him a few subtle glances while peeling oranges.

"Thought you'd like that one. I sort of grew into that boy, still running off looking for answers and—" There it was, the truth sweeping across him like icy drops of rain shaking him down to his mortal roots. He looked from the orange in his hand to Luca who snuck a slice of orange, giving him an oddly discerning look for someone so young. Jason cleared his throat again, hoping to regain some sense of not being at the whim of the Fates and deities.

"Bet you have a better story living here."

Luca laughed and in broken English told Jason a story of stealing dates, a wild chase over hills, through herds of goats, and eventually giving away his bounty to a hungry friend. It all ended with an unfortunate capture, him scrubbing his grandmother's floors, and ultimately moving in with her and enjoying a slice of buttered bread slathered with jam.

Jason couldn't stop the laughter shaking his injured shoulder, which suddenly didn't seem to hurt as bad. This, he surmised, was a life far better than he'd enjoyed in London. Simpler, truer to the eras and cultures he'd studied. Maybe if he was lucky, he'd have this with Medusa, days working on her temple, defeating a few trespassers, and a contentment and belonging he'd sought.

"I don't suppose you have any white feathers lying about?" he asked his new friend.

"Maybe." Luca stacked his bowls, having completed the orange peeling, and inclined his head back into the kitchen. Jason soon found himself with one-handed dishwashing under the supervision of Luca's particularly aggressive grandmother who, like earlier, seemed to enjoy hovering and shouting at him in Greek.

An hour later he continued with more bread kneading until Jason finally achieved that smooth dough he'd been lectured about.

"This is more like that caressing we were talking

about," he teased until Toula smacked the back of his head with a dish towel and a string of creative Greek chastising. What followed turned into a good dose of teaching the Brit about patience, bread rising, and a lesson in the proper cup of tea according to Toula. He disagreed about the tea but wisely kept that opinion to himself.

Feigning the need for fresh air and looking for something to distract him from thinking about Medusa sitting alone on her island, he offered to fix a broken shutter out front.

"You sure?" Luca asked, handing him a screwdriver.

"I'll have you know I was a sought-after odd-jobber at uni. Not to mention—" He grunted as screws came loose from the rusty hinge and the shutter hit the windowsill. Not the easiest one-handed but he was determined. "I'm not just a scholar. Did plenty of work on digs. I like getting my hands dirty." He dropped to the ground with the paint-chipped shutter and leaned it against the house.

Heat flushing his neck in the beating sun, he finished the work with little fuss.

"Ha! Easy peasy! Told you I was good." He stood back, admiring his work.

At least, until loud screeches filled the air soon followed by flapping wings.

"Cosmo," Luca shouted, laughing while Jason ducked a clearly annoyed seagull.

Apparently, Jason missed the bread crumbs littering the ground, which the winged menace soon swept down to devour. Or this was another part of his test. Bloody annoying one.

"You wanted a feather," Luca teased before waving toward the door. "Come, time for bread."

"You have no idea." Jason scooped up a feather and paused, glancing at the horizon. The sun sank lower in the sky. He tucked the feather behind his ear, the ticking away of time quickening his pace as he followed Luca into the house.

He fought back the tension, reasoning he had three things off his list. After all, he'd conquered one-handed bread making. Everything else would be easy.

Chapter Seventeen

"English." Toula confronted him full-on almost like a gorgon.

His amusement at the comparison was short lived.

Toula shoved bread wrapped in a paper bag at him. "Feed your woman and show her respect. Now go."

"Thank you for the help." He tucked the bread in his bag and slung it over his shoulder with a little help from Luca. "I don't suppose you might have a symbol of devotion you'd be willing to contribute to the cause?" He knew he was pushing his luck, but time was running short.

Toula sighed heavily before mumbling a prayer in Greek about fools and their guardians.

Luca nudged him out the front door and onto the street and patted him on the arm. "I give you this one for free. Flowers, my friend Jason." Luca disappeared back into the house before Jason could thank him.

"That was a lesson in patience and humility." He looked upward at the sky turning from blue to streaked with gold and orange. "Bet you thought I'd give up or be too up my own arse to see the lessons you think I need to learn. That's what you get wrong about me and mortal love. She's worth everything, even swallowing my pride and taking on whatever you throw at me."

A tiny competitive part of him wanted to prove that to everyone, Myrine, Eros, and the Fates. That he was clever, motivated, and not just a pathetic mortal looking for an easy way through life. Medusa was his endgame one way or another. Those thoughts quickened his steps as the day ebbed toward his deadline.

He still had two more tasks. Luca had mentioned flowers. The thing he'd once scoffed at but bought anyway for Medusa. It seemed a bit on the nose and perhaps not quite up to the Fates' standards. But as he turned the corner onto the main street, lo and behold, a flower cart sat in his path. Either this was further evidence he was no longer in control of his life, or Luca had a deal with the vendor.

He slowed to a stop at the simple wooden cart with a bright-blue umbrella protecting the colorful blooms from the sun. Flowers had symbolism that eluded him at the moment. A certain scowling frustration emerged as he scrutinized bunches of bouquets and stems of white and yellow blossoms.

"You need help picking something for your lady?" the flower woman asked, dark hair curling about her shoulders. Before he asked how she knew it was for a woman, he caught a glint of silver, a pendant against her white halter dress.

"I'll trade you for the pendent." The Greek key symbol the woman wore was a common charm found across Greece. It symbolized eternity and would fit a symbol of his devotion to Medusa, a promise of love as he'd never offered anyone. A bit over the top for him, but it fit the task.

He struggled against admitting the symbol had anything to do with welling emotions and that dull ache in the middle of his chest at the thought of never speaking to her again. Or how those same feelings drove him to pull out his empty leather wallet and add to it a crumpled folded ticket and a voucher for the local island hopper plane. The ticket wasn't anything he'd need again no matter which way this day ended.

The vendor crossed her arms and snorted. The complete opposite to the picture of a flower girl with a red blossom tucked behind her ear. Desperation pulsed in his aching shoulder. Maybe a sign from Eros pushing him to dig deeper.

"Wait." He opened his shoulder bag. Past the bread, his sketchbook, and notes, he pulled out his lucky charm, the bone carved horse.

"This may not look like much, but it's first century. Found it in a secondhand shop in London. Couldn't believe it. It's brought me good fortune. If it helps, it's for a good cause, for a woman I can't live without." He extended his hand, shaking slightly as shadows lengthened and time slipped away.

"You're the crazy tourist." She spoke in English and crossed her arms, frowning, and gave him a once-over.

"Everyone in this village really does know, don't they?" A streak of annoyance soured his mood. This wasn't just Petra the waitress calling to warn Toula to give him a hard time along with a baking lesson. Or Eros spreading gossip in his bar.

"We get lots of tourists here. Some on holiday or looking to disappear. Others prying and asking about a cursed gorgon. Most enjoy the sun, put money in our pockets, and leave. Others get what they asked for and never return."

"Except me and I'm not crazy. I came here with research and was looking for—"

"You found what you were looking for and brought

trouble. And still, you ask for more."

"I didn't bring trouble. If anything, it was already here." Snapping at the woman whose penetrating gaze nearly bored a hole in him didn't help. He was sure Myrine would hear about this, and it wasn't like he had options. Humility and desperation were not familiar emotions. But love and yearning compelled him to set aside bitterness and a need to prove himself.

"This is my last day to do right by someone who means more to me than money or possessions. I can't say I'm worthy because I'm not sure if I am. I only know I need to try, even if that means giving over to fate. Either way, you won't see me again."

"You're right, English. You're not worthy. But at least you know it. I accept your trade. Take the pendant, go, and don't come back. And stay away from my boy and mother."

Everything clicked when he accepted the pendent. Toula and Luca. He should have seen the resemblance. It was a small village after all. And Luca had sent him straight to his mother.

But it was more than a family profiting off him. The connection ran deeper. From Eros' bar, his employees, to Myrine, the clinic, Toula, and everyone around the island who never blinked an eye at his sometimes odd requests. He thought they were protecting the secret of Medusa and her island. But now he saw things differently. If they protected Medusa, why help him? Why did so many others make it to the island?

A mad thought sent a shiver down his spine. He stared at the cool silver pendent as a hypothesis settled in until he swallowed hard.

"You know about her on the island, and you've been

sending... Blimey, you're part of this."

"We honor the gods," she stated and tilted her chin up, giving him an arrogant glare worthy of Athena.

"You're filtering through tourists, choosing who to send. Sacrificing people." Teeth-gritting resentment leached into his words. He shoved the pendent into his bag and shouldered it with jerky movements that were not the best idea for his shoulder. "Including me."

That knocked his pride down a notch or two. Utter cosmic bollocks was what this was. Teaching the expert a lesson by testing and then chucking him off to be cursed, which he had, running headlong in like a lamb to slaughter. Even if it was sort of what he wanted.

"Don't you have someplace else to be?" She pulled a cover over her cart, effectively shutting down and ignoring him.

He didn't like how cold and matter-of-fact she acted. But this wasn't the time to lecture an islander on the immorality of human sacrifice. The sun grew ever closer to the horizon, and he needed to pick up the pace. He backed away from her, now seeing this place for what it was for the first time. The few pedestrians now openly stared at him. Their failed sacrifice. That did not bode well for him, and he didn't dawdle, making a beeline to Myrine.

The entire one-street town took on an ominous cast. Long shadows and suspicious glances affirmed how dangerous this place was. Part of him bellowed to stop them and expose the whole sick group.

Except that meant abandoning Medusa. If nothing else, he'd make it his mission to tell her why she had so many trespassers. She'd be pissed about the village. And if anyone could share his outrage, it was her. All the more reason he temporarily swallowed back a good moral tirade.

He picked up his pace. Heat flashed though him as he grew closer to the restaurant. His pulse began to skitter. He still had the vanity sacrifice to make. Luckily, he was clever enough to solve that one with what he still had on him.

The door was open when he approached. Tension struck through him along with caution and a need to give these people a sense of who they fucked with. Stepping into the shadowed interior of the restaurant gave him a sense of leaving the normal world behind. If a village of Hellenistic worshippers counted as normal.

"Cutting it close." Myrine sat with her sneakers propped up on a chair.

"Bread takes patience." He swept a glance at the empty restaurant.

"Show me how well you can follow directions."

Once again, he tamped down the answer he wanted to give. That led to an angry oracle and failure. Instead, he set down the paper sack on the table.

"Bread baked by my own hand."

"With help. Next." She dismissed him and crossed her arms.

"White feather." He pulled it from behind his ear and dropped it to the table. "You want me to tell you about how Luca employed a little thievery to help a friend and moved in with his grandmother?"

"I'll give you that one on credit. Symbol of devotion?"

He gently laid out the Greek key charm. "The eternity I would give her if I could."

"And vanity?" she asked, leaning forward on the

table.

"I'll be cutting my hair and making a proper vanity sacrifice." He was feeling right chuffed at his success.

"Oh, come on, Jason!" Eros appeared from a dark corner. "Hair is so two thousand years ago. A weak offering and way too easy for the miracle you're about to receive. I'm not buying it, and neither will the Fates. I mean look in a mirror. For someone who says he's vain about his hair… Well, let's just say grooming is not your strength." He preened, running a hand through his perfectly styled golden hair.

"Bollocks!" All thought of deference and winning favor vanished. Manly indignation roared through Jason. "Plenty of women find me and my hair noteworthy. It's not like I lacked dates. And Medusa is very fond of… Well, she likes it. This isn't London. I don't have to be quaffed and professional. It's an island getaway. The beach look is in."

Of all the petty, shallow, and very Olympian prejudiced complaints. Every muscle locked into battle mode. Even his protesting shoulder matched his mood.

"I'm not wrong, and we don't have to do this. You can walk away now, alone."

"I'm so done with this." Myrine stood with a tinkling of her many charmed bracelets.

"No, wait," Jason grudgingly said with rough exasperation. He hadn't come this far to give up. "I'm sorry, and I don't want to walk away. This isn't even about me."

"I'll accept an apology for the vast amount of insult you just laid out." Eros slowly circled Jason like a predator. "And this is about you. Vanity, my lad. That's what gets you what you want if you still want it bad enough."

"I've been shot, doused with flour, chastised by the baker, shown up by a kid, and learned this entire island is apparently making sacrifices by sending tourists for Medusa to off. All of which has shown me up. I don't have much vanity left."

Eros snorted in laughter, stretching Jason's patience. He kept reminding himself all of this would lead him back to Medusa who would probably give him an outraged lecture and then laugh.

"Gods, he's not getting it." Myrine slapped her hands against her hips. "Vanity is personal, and yours hasn't got anything to do with appearance." She shook her head, dismay rolling off her pink cardigan-covered shoulders. "Look, fixing the outside isn't my area, but don't think I won't send you off to that island without some decent grooming products. Now try again, English."

"Jason, come on," Eros cajoled and slapped down a familiar manila envelope.

"That's my journal and work to be sent back to London—" The truth slammed Jason in the chest with the force of the bullet that put a hole in his shoulder. Tricky immortals.

"It's a small price to pay for an end to loneliness and for someone who loves you without all that distraction of the modern world."

"The sun is setting," Myrine reminded him. "Choose your path. I've got an engagement party to bless."

There it was, sitting before him in nauseatingly normal paper. His work, the achievement of a lifetime, respect, and bloody proving he was right to all those who called him a dreamer lacking conviction and discipline.

Accolades and recognition or love. The obvious choice hurt his ego to let it go, but what was ego compared to waking up every morning cradled in the warmth of a woman who made him laugh and understood him better than anyone?

They called it sacrifice. Banished to a stone temple. He'd take it if it meant spending days with her, living in the world he'd studied and admired. That made this last tribute easier.

When he lifted the envelope, it didn't seem so heavy now, even filled with paper and digital records. "Vanity, the work of a lifetime."

"And how much life did you give up for that vanity?"

He glanced at Eros, looking so human and yet not. He still kicked himself at how blind he'd been. "You know, for the god of love, sometimes I think you miss what us mortals want."

"And what's that?"

"Someone who understands who you are and loves the parts of you that even you don't. She has her snakes, and I have mine even if you can't see them."

He walked over to a plate of candles, held the envelope over the flames, and closed his eyes. He thought of Medusa, her warm-as-treacle voice, holding her, and the comfort and peace of her presence, and let go of what had driven his life.

When he opened his eyes, flames consumed everything he had held dear in a very mythological white-hot flash that singed his fingers.

"Now there is only one thing left," Myrine announced at his side.

Jason yanked his hand back, blowing on his fingers

while the charred cinders of a life he'd left blew away on a breeze.

"The true act of devotion and love." Eros squeezed his good shoulder. "Go to her, free from this world, take that last step, and accept who she is, all of her, the part she's kept hidden."

Funny, out of all the things they asked, gazing upon the woman he loved, facing her curse, was the least difficult part.

Of course, Eros pulled out all the stops with a wave of his hand, plunging them into darkness.

"Good luck, Jason Walker." Myrine's words echoed as if they were in a tunnel. The darkness in the café pressed in around him until shadows thickened and turned pitch black. A gust of wind carried the scent of the sea. In one dizzying snap, he found himself on that fateful rickety wooden pier with moonlight dancing on the sea.

"This is where I leave you." Eros stood by him, still dressed as the mortal but again, solemn, almost as if he were the one taking the plunge into an unknown destiny.

The rhythmic sound of paddle dipping into water was followed by the shadow of the ferryman slowly moving toward them.

"I guess if I survive, it's your greatest triumph." Jason broke the quiet between them.

"With an attitude like that, you'll ruin it for both of us. Go snog her and have hot gorgon love. And remember, I get a tribute of thanks that will make its way to even the stingiest ears on Olympus."

"Deal," Jason agreed and held out his hand, which Eros clamped on to firmly. Maybe he should be more nervous. The favor he'd been granted, or earned really, was a bit odd. In some twisted way, he almost felt like it went deeper. Maybe everyone misunderstood Eros. He'd certainly find out soon enough from Medusa.

"Thank you."

"Go on. Long goodbyes make me ill." He shoved Jason toward the sighing ferryman.

"One last trip, eh, mate?" Jason teased as he climbed onto the ferry.

"With you, I doubt it."

"Not this time." Jason sat back and let the shadows wrap around him. The shore disappeared into the darkness, and he allowed the lap of water and the moon sparkling on the waves to ease away worries and the life he left behind. Perhaps, if he allowed himself to embrace the Fates, Eros, and everything they represented, he could hear a hint of his mother's approval carrying across the water.

"I'm coming home," he promised Medusa and himself.

Chapter Eighteen

Medusa curled up next to a column, overlooking the sea, barely moving all day. The air in the temple seemed heavy and oppressive, humidity seeping through her gown. Even her snakes seemed subdued and lethargic, barely a hiss escaping.

The quiet before a storm. Time slowed and moved as fast as honey on a cool day. Gods, but the waiting, the overthinking every word Eros and Hermes spoke about Jason, was agonizing as if time itself tore at her bare skin.

The sun sank low, painting the sky in pinks and yellows as if soothing her. Soon, even the sky faded into darkness. Another day gone. Eventually, she stood, walking into the temple to endure another lonely night and only the flickering of the lit braziers to keep her warm. She poured the last of the wine from the picnic basket Jason had left. It barely touched the tide of melancholy dragging at her.

Tossing aside the empty goblet until it thudded and rolled across the sandy floor, she slowly meandered through the crumbling remains of her victims, the statues of the vanquished, until she reached her curtained alcove. Dark and vacant as her heart. Just as she settled into another night of staring and thinking about how her life couldn't get any worse, those damn temple bells chimed.

Of course. Really, she'd brought it on herself with the whole what-could-be-worse musing.

"Halt, trespasser. To enter this temple means to face your doom." She could barely work up the enthusiasm. Her delivery was less than ominous. This one she'd end quickly and then curl down for a good post-curse cry and pity party.

"Am I still a trespasser? I thought we'd sort of gotten beyond that."

"Jason." He'd come back. Tears burned her eyes as her heart nearly burst. She made to rush forward in a grand romantic reunion until cold reality doused her in the icy bucket of repercussions and godly favors with strings attached.

"I know you sent me away to live. But I couldn't. You know me, stubborn scribe, sets his mind to find Medusa, falls madly for her. Spent a couple of days in a hospital, had some time to think. Well, maybe had a certain god and oracle insulting me until I had to admit a few things."

Jason's footsteps echoed as he grew closer to where she, in her fear, had stopped to question his life choices. Hers as well.

"What things?" She winced at not asking if he was well. The man had nearly bled out on her temple floor. She risked inching closer to him, catching a glimpse of a white shirt hanging loose over long jean-clad legs.

"Oh, you know, the usual tosh. My life since my parents died. Burying myself in work. Avoiding relationships and running away from everything and everyone. Except you."

She sucked her bottom lip, nervously straightening her gown, which was a mess if she was honest. Why hadn't she changed her gown and bathed instead of lingering in a state of dejection and pining?

He stopped a half-dozen steps from her, hair pulled back and tied at the nape of his neck. She caught a whiff of fresh-baked bread mixed with sandalwood. So tempting. She had to dig deep inside herself for the ironclad will not to rush him and bury her face in his neck. Or other more interesting places. Her snakes whispered in agreement. Probably a sign she should stop this now before she broke her heart any more.

"It's not a bad thing to think about your mistakes. Now that you see where things went wrong, you can go back to your life and make changes." Every word was like scalding-hot oil torturing herself with what was best for him. Even now, with every sense in her body yearning for his touch, she couldn't bear to ruin him with her cursed life.

"Oh, love, I am fixing it. I'm here. That life, it was never right for me no matter how hard I tried. My brother always fit, even leaving me and my parents behind. I realize it now, Mum and Dad lived their passion, and none of what the rest of the world thought mattered. They lived and died for what made them happiest, being together, sharing discovery and knowledge. I've been searching for that, and I finally found it with you, here."

"But you can't. You're mortal, and my curse will cnd you. And I'm so afraid, Jason. I can't kill the man I love. I'd become the monster your people think I am." Choking tears stole her breath. Curling up in a weeping ball on the floor wasn't exactly what the fearsome gorgon should do. She remained as still as her stone statues, afraid to move and cause what she feared most.

"I'm told I need to get over myself, to trust and have faith. Never had much faith, me. I was good with following the clues left behind by the old world, poems, inscriptions, epic stories, and archaeological evidence. Years, I spent piecing it together until I formed opinions I wanted to prove. Hard evidence, that was my religion. None of that was fulfilling. What's it all mean without someone to share it with?"

If it were possible, she cried harder until her snakes seemed to hiss in tandem with her sobs. Gods, she would not survive this. Him, her hardened, grumbly Jason, tossed out of her temple and kept coming back, now with romantic declarations so monumental, they must shake the foundations of Olympus. As she snorted and coughed back her tears, she couldn't help but think Eros must be toasting his success. Except it wasn't, not really.

"I know what you're thinking." He turned slightly toward her, shadows teasing her with glimpses of his face. "It's not all Eros, although I do owe him. Promised him we'd light a lantern in thanks and made sure we gave him proper tribute."

He took a few steps forward, hand held out in front of him, and for a moment, her throat closed up. Was he blind? Had they taken his sight, his beautiful eyes? She shrank a few steps back. Coward her, not wanting to know if that was his fate but unable to force him away. Neither of them could go on like this, drawn together and shoved apart, living in fear and at the mercy of others. That brought another wave of hot agony ripping her apart.

"Whatever he promised you, he can't unmake my curse or make you immune from it. Tell me he didn't blind you." She could barely ask, her voice growing hoarse.

"Not blind and you're right. He couldn't do all that. That would take an act of higher power," Jason agreed.

"You went to the Fates. That was dangerous, and you shouldn't have." She couldn't help but groan and fret.

"I'm honestly a little hurt you think I can't talk my way to a favor with the Fates."

"Jason, you sweet, deluded scribe, you are a talented artist and historian but—" She sighed, possibly a little more dramatically than she should have, but he deserved it. "Respectfully petitioning deities is not what I would call your strength."

"I can be nice. When the situation calls for it. The oracle, she was a bit on the petulant side, but we reached an understanding."

"What did they ask you to do or sacrifice?" A headache throbbed behind her eyes, and yes, she'd gone from happy weeping to fear to now plain tired of wondering what her adorable, clueless scribe had done.

"Nothing much. Although baking bread one-handed and talking Toula into helping me was a challenge."

He had that rough amusement lilting in his voice that would, under other circumstances, have left her smiling and teasing him. However, not when his life was on the line. Or when her gorgon senses sizzled and snapped, leaving her on the cusp of ranting about Olympian mischief. Instead, she focused on one detail, determined to extract what he wasn't telling her.

"Toula," she stated in flat disbelief. "And this Toula helped you make bread?"

"More like gave a lesson in her kitchen, her and her grandson, Luca. Had to clean dishes and then there was the jam making. Wasn't so bad by the end." He felt his way around a statue, working through the temple closer to her.

"What aren't you telling me?" She sighed and paced in a small circle, waiting for the proverbial drachma or maybe a few hundred of them to drop. He wasn't that far from her. She could easily storm over and kiss him into telling her.

"Love, I promise no blood was spilled. The only thing exchanged was my dignity in the kitchen, a story from my past, which was oddly therapeutic, symbolic evidence of my devotion, and a sacrifice of vanity."

"What sacrifice? What did you do?" Yes, she shouted. Her hands curled into fists she wanted to beat on a column.

"I'm not answering until you're here with me." He held out a hand in the opposite direction of where she stood, which proved her suspicion he was trying to soothe her with closed eyes.

"I am here, just like I always am. And you know I can't be with you unless you have that blindfold."

"This faith thing applies to both of us."

"Well, that's a load of—" She made a frustrated groan instead of the very unkind things she'd like to say. No sense in tempting the wrath of the gods. He talked of faith like all it took was accepting. To her, faith was a trick used by the gods to cause the greatest pain possible.

"My eyes are closed, and I'm not opening them until we get through this last faith part. It's been a long day, and I may fall asleep. Unless someone wants to give me a reason to stay awake. I believe the fairy tales do this with a kiss."

"I'm not a fairy tale."

"No, you're a flesh-and-blood woman, a powerful gorgon who made me feel alive and excited to bring you flowers and chocolates. You're not a monster, but you are the woman I love. Please tell me we've gotten past the uncomfortable declarations and my baring myself before you and the universe."

"I'm afraid." She spoke her fear softly, overwhelmed by a wave of yearning for him, for this chance he was willing to sacrifice his life for.

"That's what some of them on Olympus want. It gives them power."

She softly approached behind him. "Tell me what you sacrificed."

"Love, it's Eros we're talking about here, so he gave me one of the classics. Vanity. I tried to cut off my hair as an offering, and he—"

"No!" She didn't mean to squawk like that and wrapped her arms around his waist. "I mean, I would've sort of missed that."

His hand, warm and strong, covered hers. "Lucky for you, both the oracle and Eros rejected my brilliant plan." His voice was light and teasing again. "They saw more about me than I did."

"So what did you sacrifice?"

"My life's work, everything that brought me here, the proof that would have been published if I died."

"But that's your leverage against them." Her ears rang with the significance of what he'd done. "They could betray you. You'll look at me and die."

"That's where the faith part comes in. The cost of a favor asked. The part where I prove why I want this, what I'm willing to do, and who gets credit for two people who should never meet, much less fall in love and find happiness together."

"You believe them." She gasped softly, her chest flushing hot after his declarations of love.

185

"I know how it sounds." He laughed in a short burst. "Me, Mr. Anti-romance, nose stuck in my research, barmy professor on a mission, now ready for a lifetime commitment. Never saw this coming but that's sort of the point." He slowly twisted in her arms.

Every muscle locked in place until a slight tremor coursed through her. Tears wet her eyes and fell down her cheeks. Breathing was long since forgotten until a dizziness zinged through her. "Jason, I—" Air was necessary, and she inhaled deeply, now staring at how his face relaxed, eyes closed in a peace she wanted to share.

His one arm was still bandaged in a sling, now between them. His other hand cradled her cheek, and she tried not to swoon into his touch and the light caress of his thumb across her lips.

"This is my choice, not anyone else's."

She took him in from graying brows, strong jaw showing a slight prickle of stubble, giving him that rugged handsome look. All she wanted was to snuggle against his chest and beg him not to do this. Yet the tranquility and acceptance surrounding him stopped her.

He slowly dropped his hand to her hip. "Are you ready, love?" His voice turned warm and husky, melting away fear until she was again a soft, young girl in love.

Her snakes didn't whip or thrash as they did during her curse. It was like they were waiting.

"When I look, all I'll see is the eyes of the woman I love."

"I want you to." Her voice shook, and tears coursed down her face in salty rivers. And she prayed then, to Eros, the Fates, and all of Olympus, promising to fulfill her charge if they would let him live. Give her this one thing for the brave mortal who believed in them and now kept their secret in his heart, the same heart he shared with her.

"Kiss me first," she demanded, channeling the strength he seemed to think she had.

Gasping against firm lips, she drew his bottom lip in and moaned his name. Nothing in the five mortal realms beat kissing him, with each subtle glide of his lips and curl of his tongue. He cradled her neck, drawing her against him, warm and cajoling, playfully nibbling and bouncing his nose against hers until they both pulled apart, and he rested his forehead against hers.

"Let me see you," he said, drawing the words out.

She raised her eyes and watched his open. Her breath caught at deep blue broken by dark pupils boring into her.

"You're beautiful." His voice cracked, and then it all went to Hades.

She tried to jerk away as power burned across her skin. Her snakes thrashed and hissed words she couldn't make out but feared.

"No one ever described your eyes, like a sunset on the ocean." He gasped, and his head jerked back.

"Jason!"

His hand dug into her shoulder as he convulsed until he fell to his knees. She sank down with him. Jagged sobs shook her body as singeing heat raced through her. Dust rained down, and a crack of thunder shook the temple. Sweat beaded on her skin as a fire seemed to consume both them. As long as they went together, she embraced it.

Except no flames or burning anything rained down on them. His grunts and screams silenced. Quiet descended like a stillness from the grave. Jason had rolled away from her, but she still clamped her fingers into his waist.

She blinked and swiped at her snakes acting limp and lethargic. An ocean breeze swept through the temple, cooling her skin. Disbelief carved away pain and fear at how they'd lived through whatever in Tartarus just happened to them. She rubbed dust from her eyes until her gaze landed on Jason's unmoving form, facedown and covered in a fine layer of dust.

"Jason." She reached for his shoulder, barely covered by a tattered shirt.

Wait. Bare muscular shoulder, not injured.

"Well, this is weird." He coughed and rolled over to face her.

"Holy Gods," she whispered as her formerly mortal scribe now gazed at her with blue eyes flecked with gold and hair now writhing with silver-gray striped snakes. "You're—"

"Yeah, snakes kind of itch. Still, could've been worse." He traced his fingers across her cheek. "You look like you need a bath."

She gaped before a snorting giggle burst out. "Such a smooth-talking gorgon. I'm all atwitter for all those compliments."

"What? You don't want me to sweep my lovely lady off to a bath where I can worship her properly, with compliments like how no artist would capture eyes as rich as a sunset. Or maybe trace the strong regal curve of her cheek, as beautiful as Nefertiti and just as powerful."

She stilled his fingers, taking in his long lean form, muscles rippling under warm tanned skin as if he'd been worshipping the sun even though she knew he'd been ill.

"How do you feel?" She sat up on her knees, and he matched her, lacing his fingers with hers.

"Tired but still buzzing with whatever happened." He reached one hand to his head. One of his snakes hissed before wrapping around his fingers. He blinked, and a smile emerged, dimpling his cheeks. "How do I look?" His smile slipped.

"Fishing for compliments?" she teased.

His face flushed, and he shrugged, dropping his hand to cup hers. "No, I—" He gazed over her shoulder, his eyes widening as he looked into the moonlight filtering into the temple. "I can see so much more. Even at night the colors are so vibrant. Guess I don't need the glasses anymore. Quite a perk, this."

She'd never thought how she perceived the world would be different. In that moment, the depth of this gift, of Jason, hit her full force. They had so much to learn from each other, to share.

Unable to contain the rush of emotions, she tackled him, burying her face in his neck until her snakes hissed in outrage before tangling with his in a joining she hoped to share. "I love you so much. Tell me you don't regret this. I'm so afraid you'll hate me for how your life is changed, and now you're stuck here with me."

"No regrets. And what I've gained is so much more than what I left behind," he crooned.

She melted a little inside. Especially how he drew his hand down her back.

"Could use that bath, though."

"For two?" she teased, nipping at his earlobe, unable to contain the desire flushing through her after a harrowing night and morning.

"Well, I do need someone to teach me how to care

for the new hair style and how to be a hot gorgon."

Laughter turned into a girlish squeal as he swept her up in his arms bridal style. Gazing into his eyes, she said a prayer of thanks to all the gods in the pantheon. Two thousand years had been a heavy price to pay, but if this was her reward, it was worth it.

"It's good to be home," he affirmed, and with the assured swagger of a man who had his gorgon, he strode into the heart of the temple, into their alcove, and the start of a new myth. Medusa and her gorgon husband, the sometimes monsters but always lovers.

A word about the author...

A Floridian by birth, I now call the mountains of North Georgia my home. Along with two sometimes loud and demanding cats, I work mostly from home, navigating legal documents and various aspects of the US legal system.

Although a paralegal by day, I am a lifetime addict of the science fiction and paranormal romance genres. I read my first romance in high school and immediately worked my way through various series until it only made sense for me to work at the used bookstore I spent so much time in.

Storytelling and writing came a decade later after volunteering for a service organization as a docent for a historical cemetery tour. Suddenly, I was diving into researching the stories of the dead and leading tours and writing some of my own script.

Jump ahead another ten years. After losing my mother, I made a life-changing move to the mountains of North Georgia where I found my muse and wrote as voraciously as I read. A few trips to London and suddenly werewolves, mythological characters, witches, and mages had taken up residence in my head and on my laptop. With permission of my resident furry taskmasters, of course.

~*~

Find Lianne Kelly online at:
http://liannekelly.com